"Amy," Hugh said softly, touching her arm. *"Wake up. It's late. It's time you were in bed."*

She stirred slightly. The only sign she'd heard him was a faint fluttering of the dark eyelashes resting on her pale cheeks. "Amy…"

This time she mumbled and tried to turn over. Sleepy brown eyes looked up into his face. "Hugh," she said with a soft smile lighting up her face. "You're back."

And he wanted to kiss her.

What was happening to him? He'd known Amy for years and never felt the slightest inclination to do anything of the sort. He'd picked her up when she'd fallen off her horse at fourteen and broken her wrist without the slightest stirring of the emotions troubling him now. Even when he'd held her while she sobbed at her mother's funeral he hadn't felt the stirrings of any attraction. This was *Amy.*

From city girl—to corporate wife!

Working side by side, nine to five—and beyond....
No matter how hard these couples try to keep their
relationships strictly professional, romance is
definitely on the agenda!

But will a date in the office diary lead to
an appointment at the altar?

Next month, don't miss:
The Corporate Marriage Campaign
by Leigh Michaels
Harlequin Romance #3857

THE BUSINESS ARRANGEMENT

Natasha Oakley

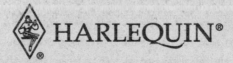

TORONTO • NEW YORK • LONDON
AMSTERDAM • PARIS • SYDNEY • HAMBURG
STOCKHOLM • ATHENS • TOKYO • MILAN • MADRID
PRAGUE • WARSAW • BUDAPEST • AUCKLAND

ISBN 0-373-03854-2

THE BUSINESS ARRANGEMENT

First North American Publication 2005.

CHAPTER ONE

'WHAT do you mean "no"? Come on, Amy,' Hugh coaxed, stretching his arm out along the back of the floral-patterned sofa. 'I need your help.'

Amelia Mitchell scarcely looked up from the book she was reading, merely pulling her legs tightly under her and snuggling deeper into the cushioned window-seat. 'I'm sure you don't. Not really. There must be someone else you can ask.'

'I've asked you.'

'Sorry, no can do.'

'Why can't you? You're not working at the moment.'

'That's not the point, though, is it?' she replied, risking a look up at Hugh Balfour's confidently smiling face. The assurance in his voice had been irritating, but his expression made her angry. Clearly he felt he needed only to exude some of his well-documented charm and she'd crumble. 'I don't want to.'

'Why?'

'Because I'd hate it. You'd be horrid. I'd be bored. If I wanted to be your secretary I'd apply for the job.' She uncurled and threw her book to one side. 'Actually I can't think of anything worse. I'm angry with Seb for having suggested it.'

'He was trying to help.'

'Help *who* exactly?' she asked, turning to face him, all five feet two inches bristling with indignation. *This was just typical!* 'I know you two go back a long way, but I'm his *sister*. You'd think he'd put me before his friend.'

Even as she said it she knew it was nonsense. Seb wouldn't see anything wrong in offering his sister's help to his best friend, however inconvenient it might be to the sister. She loved him to pieces, but he'd never yet considered her feelings or appeared to notice any of the sacrifices she'd made.

It hadn't even occurred to him that he ought to let his sister know he was coming to stay this weekend for the annual regatta. If challenged, he would, no doubt, say he'd a perfect right to be there since he owned a third share in their mother's Henley-on-Thames cottage. But it would have been nice if he'd made a courtesy telephone call. Remembered the seventeenth-century cottage they'd inherited was her home.

Hugh's long fingers traced a small circle on the mahogany table by his side; he was completely unfazed by her outburst. 'It's only for a couple of weeks. Think of the money. I'll pay well.'

'Don't need any.'

'You must be the first student to say so.'

'I'm not a student any more. Fully fledged BA (Hons)—'

'Currently unemployed.'

She shot him a look of dislike. 'With no ambitions to be a secretary and certainly not yours.'

'Amy, please. I really do need your help,' he said, flashing her a crooked smile, his eyes lighting up with an irrepressible glint of pure sex appeal.

As her stomach twisted in recognition it crossed her mind to wonder whether anyone had been able to refuse Hugh Balfour anything. His mother certainly hadn't. He was her shining blue-eyed boy, one without blemish.

Amy could have enlightened her, as could the numerous ex-girlfriends he'd dumped with ruthless expediency at the first hint of boredom. Six feet high with the muscle tone of a natural sportsman and the kind of charisma that made everyone follow his lead, Hugh was blessed with more gifts than it was fair for one man to possess.

Nevertheless he'd some serious character flaws. Flaws encouraged, no doubt, by getting his own way on practically every occasion since birth. It was just difficult to remember them when you faced the full force of Hugh's charm—particularly when he normally reserved it for women with legs up to their armpits and a chiselled bone structure.

Which actually made this whole situation rather funny when she came to think about it. Hugh must really be desperate if he was spending so much time on Seb's little sister. He hadn't done that since he'd broken the Rev. Adderton's window with a cricket ball and had persuaded her not to tell. Her lips twitched. 'More.'

'More what?' he asked, confused.

'Don't stop there. I'm enjoying seeing you beg.'

'If that's what it takes I will.' He smiled slowly, the grooves in his cheeks deepening. 'Sweet Amy—'

'Don't overdo it. I'm beginning to feel queasy.'

Hugh relaxed back in his chair, evidently certain of success. 'As soon as Seb suggested it I knew you'd be perfect. And before you get angry again he wasn't thinking about it as a job opportunity. It's more…about protecting me.'

'From what?' As if she needed to ask. Hugh's problems only ever involved women and this would be no exception. 'If you want my help you're going to have to tell me what's really going on. Go on, tell the truth.'

'The truth?'

She folded her arms in front of her. 'If you can manage it. Look, if you just needed a secretary while your PA's away you could ring an agency or borrow someone from another department. I'm not a complete idiot.'

He smiled. 'I never thought you were. The truth is...sensitive information.'

'Surprise me.'

'If I get someone in from an agency I can't rely on them not to...gossip.' Hugh paused again, unusually having to search for his words.

'About?' she prompted, watching his face closely. Normally Hugh was the archetypal Mr Smooth. Always in control. But something had really got to him this time.

'I'm hoping to avoid anyone knowing...' He petered out again, his eyes flicking past her to look down the long cottage garden.

'About?' Amy repeated without relenting.

'About...a woman—'

'Ah.'

He shot her a look of irritation. 'I don't know what you mean by "Ah". There's no "Ah" about it. This has never happened to me before and I'm running out of ideas on how to contain...the problem.'

'A problem with a woman?' Amy leant forward and gracefully crossed her legs, mockingly adopting the pose of a therapist. It was getting better every moment. It was about time some woman somewhere managed to strike a blow for the rest of their kind.

She liked Hugh. She'd always liked Hugh. He was great fun. Interesting to talk to. But he treated women with all the careless contempt given to a disposable tissue and there was something truly satisfying in seeing him rocked off balance. She nodded with her head tilted onto one side. 'How surprising. Go on.'

Hugh rubbed his left shoulder in a vain attempt to ease the knotting muscle forming there. When Seb had first mooted the idea of his sister taking the temporary vacancy in his office he'd conveniently forgotten how exasperating Amy could be.

She *could* type, she *was* loyal and she was almost *family*, for heaven's sake. They were all great credentials for what he needed, but he'd completely overlooked her irritating habit of laughing at him. All the time. And this situation with Richard's wife was becoming anything but funny.

On the other hand Amy was still his best option. In fact, she was his only option. He took a deep breath. 'This...woman telephones, sends...letters and...gifts to me at the office. She's m—'

'Married! I can guess,' Amy interrupted, standing up swiftly. 'I'm not doing it! You get yourself out of your own muddles. I'm not sitting about your office lying for you.'

'I—'

'You should have known I wouldn't do anything to help you break up anyone's marriage. After everything I've seen—'

'Will you shut up and listen? It's difficult enough without you interrupting all the time. Sit down and let me explain.'

'Go on, then,' she said ungraciously, sitting back down in a chair opposite him and tracing the pattern on the carpet with the edge of her shoe.

'That's why I need your help. I'm not doing it either.'

She looked up, a slight frown between her eyebrows. 'Not doing what? I don't understand. Wh—?'

'Married women have never been my thing, Amy. And even if they were there's no way I'd be tempted by this one.'

'So what's the problem?'

His blue eyes met her brown ones. 'Trying to get Sonya Laithwaite to accept the fact,' he stated baldly, watching closely for her reaction.

Amy's lips opened and closed a couple of times before she managed to repeat, *'Sonya Laithwaite?'*

Hugh sat back. At least he'd finally got her attention.

Hell, this was so much more awkward than he'd ever imagined. He hated even saying the woman's name. Hated thinking what it would do to Richard if he discovered what his wife was up to—and with whom. He doubted his relationship with the older man would survive it.

And that mattered to him. Richard was so much more than his employer. He'd been there at all the difficult turning points of his life, helped guide his future, and as Hugh had grown to adulthood they'd become friends. Nothing could have been more calculated to hurt Richard than what Sonya was doing.

Hugh watched Amy's mouth move pointlessly a couple more times before saying dryly, 'Stop doing a fish impersonation. This is serious, Amy. I really do *need* your help.'

It brought her up short. 'Sonya *Laithwaite*? My godfather's wife?'

Hugh nodded.

'B-but…but they only married last May.'

'And she's bored already and looking for entertainment,' he said, standing up and pacing towards the window. He could feel her eyes on his back watching him. Judging him. 'Honestly, Amy,' he said, turning suddenly, 'as God's my witness I've not done anything to encourage her…' He trailed off and thrust an angry hand through his hair.

Without any difficulty Amy conjured an image of Sonya in her mind's eye. Apart from the wedding itself, when she'd worn a white puff-ball dress with far too much diamante, the one and only time Amy had seen her had been at her father's house-warming party the previous autumn and she'd made a colourful impression.

A full-frontal assault of a redhead in baby pink with a bust that could take your eye out if she turned suddenly and you hadn't seen her coming. She wasn't the kind of woman who'd need much encouragement for anything, judging from the way she'd danced with Seb. But even so there must have been something. Something Hugh'd done to convince her he was interested.

It didn't bear thinking about. He owed Richard Laithwaite so much. When Hugh's father had died it had been Richard, a childhood friend of both their mothers, who'd come alongside the bewildered twelve-year-old boy and filled the void. *How could Hugh even think of repaying him like that?*

'You can't have an affair with Sonya. You can't do that to Richard. He believed in you, mentored you in the beginning. I don't believe even you would sink so low.'

'*Exactly.* That's what I've been saying. I can't. Even if I wanted to, I wouldn't,' he said, meeting her eyes with a steely determination.

She pulled at the gold chain round her neck. 'You don't want to?'

'No.'

His reply had been unequivocal but she looked a little doubtful. Men did go for women like Sonya, after all, and Hugh was more easily distracted by the next pair of legs than most. 'You're not even a little bit tempted?'

'Of course not. *She's Richard's wife.* I do think he's been a complete idiot to marry a woman twenty-seven years younger than himself—particularly one like Sonya. I also believe she'll find someone who'll eagerly take up her offer sooner rather than later. But I'm equally certain it won't be me. You must have a really low opinion of me to think I'd even contemplate treating him like that,' he said on a final, sudden spurt of anger.

Amy was unmoved. She smiled sunnily across at the harsh expression on his handsome face, finally convinced. 'When it comes to women it couldn't be lower. I'd have thought Sonya's obvious attractions might hold some fascination for you,' she said angelically, thinking of the bouncing thirty-four DDs the redhead displayed in dresses apparently spray-painted on.

'Would you?' he bit out dangerously.

Amy stopped her laugh in her throat and it came out as a husky chuckle. 'Obviously not. Truthfully I've never given your preferences much thought. A leg man, are you?' she quipped, faltering slightly beneath the quelling look in his eyes. 'Have you considered just telling her you're not interested? You know, just saying it straight out?'

His eyes conveyed eloquently what he thought of that suggestion. 'Sonya believes I'm being noble.'

'Then she doesn't know you very well!' she cut in, trying to stop the bubble of amusement bursting out of control.

'Stop it, Amy. It isn't funny. She's convinced herself I feel guilty about Richard. That the only thing stopping me grabbing what's on offer is fear of what other people think.'

'There's a fair bit to grab.' She couldn't resist chipping in with a swipe at the woman's cosmetically enhanced assets before adding carelessly, 'Oh, just tell her you don't go for married women. Tell her it's too complicated to get involved with your boss's wife.'

If only it had been that simple. Hugh thought back over the numerous conversations he'd had with Sonya and wondered how much of them to tell Amy. He turned back from the window and sat down. 'It's not that easy. If I speak to her she takes it as encouragement. Whatever I've tried has been a disaster. She doesn't give up.'

Amy frowned at the suddenly weary tone in his voice, her desire to laugh evaporating. 'Are you trying to tell me she's stalking you?'

'I'm not sure how you define "stalking",' he hedged. 'I don't imagine she's dangerous, but what I'm trying to say is she's making my life a damned misery. My PA's been fantastic. When we've known Sonya's in the building Barbara's worked late so we could leave together. If I'm in the office all day she's brought sandwiches to eat at her desk. Just brilliant. With her away, I'm just too vulnerable.'

'Couldn't an agency temp do all that?' Amy asked, biting on her finger.

'Only if I explained what was happening. Sonya's the chief executive's wife, for heaven's sake. She's in the building all the time. What possible excuse could I give for not wanting to be left alone with her?'

Amy blew her fringe off her face. There wasn't one. There was no plausible explanation except the truth, and if he confided in a temporary secretary it would probably travel round Harpur-Laithwaite like wildfire. 'How long has it been going on?' she asked at last.

'Just a couple of months. Three perhaps. I didn't think too much about it at first. There was nothing for a few days and then maybe two small incidents in the same day. She's always been a bit…overt.'

'I can imagine.' Her voice was dry. 'Go on. There must have been a trigger. Something that started it all getting more serious.'

He'd thought along those lines himself, going back over the occasions he'd been in Sonya's company and trying to pinpoint the moment she'd begun to pursue him with the tenacity of a terrier.

But there was nothing. Nothing concrete anyway. His suspicions were all based on conjecture and almost unthinkable.

'I can't think of any one single incident to explain it. I think she must feel trapped. Perhaps she sees my lifestyle and wants it.'

Amy's mouth twisted in wry humour. Somehow she doubted Hugh's lifestyle was the draw. Richard Laithwaite was a lovely man. He'd been a part of Amy's childhood since she could remember, always an unfailing source of ice-cream and surprisingly able to read *Winnie the Pooh* better than anyone else she knew. But marriage to him? *No!* It wasn't something she'd ever have contemplated.

No one had been in any doubt why Sonya had chosen to marry him—money. Years and years of focusing exclusively on the acquisition of it had made Richard fabulously wealthy. Why he'd suddenly decided to abandon his single life was more of a mystery.

And now Sonya was bored. She had the designer clothes, the beautiful car, the Elizabethan manor house in Oxfordshire and it wasn't quite enough. And then there was Hugh. However much Amy would like to bring Hugh Balfour down a peg or seven she had to admit he was a tempting alternative. Young and gorgeous with incredible eyes. Deep, deep blue with a hint of devilment. Pure sex and almost irresistible. To be immune to Hugh you had to know him very well indeed.

Poor Richard. Her heart ached for him when she imagined the pain he'd go through if he discovered how Sonya felt about Hugh. He loved Hugh like the son he'd never made time to have. It would be the ultimate betrayal.

'What are you going to do?' she asked quietly.

'Wait. Just for a while. I'm confident I can sort it, but I need Richard to be safely away from office gossip and that's why I need you.' Hugh allowed himself a half-smile. 'Sonya's dubbed Barbara my "Rottweiler" and convinced herself I'm inhibited by my PA's antagonism.'

'And you think I'd make a good guard dog? Thanks, I think.'

Hugh's smile widened as he took in the determined tilt of her chin completely undermined by a freckle-covered nose and the strands of fine, flyaway hair escaping from her pony-tail. 'I think you've got potential as a Rottweiler pup. More importantly I trust you not to say anything.' He hesitated before adding, 'And if I'm going for complete honesty here, it's not just Richard's feelings I'm worried about.'

'What do you mean?'

'I think Sonya has it in her to be vengeful. I'm going to have to be quite brutal with her in the end, and if I'm alone with her at all there's the danger of people believing anything she might choose to say about me. Even if she weren't believed implicitly there'd be the assumption I must have encouraged her. Much as you thought—and you know how much I think of Richard.'

'I didn't say that exactly.'

'Yes, you did. Anyway, it's a risk I don't want to take. Not if I can help it. And until Richard has retired I want to play it softly. I don't want him hurt and I don't want my reputation mired up with anything quite so distasteful.'

Amy struggled to take it all in. She pushed up the sleeves of her jumper and hugged her knees. Her knowledge of Sonya was scanty, but she was unquestionably the type to be vindictive when she realised that Hugh, who seemed to have slept with half of London over the years, was drawing the line at her. 'I can see you need someone,' she said doubtfully. 'I just don't think I'm a very good idea. I'm not a properly trained secretary.'

Hugh jumped at the blatant sign of weakening and pushed home his advantage. 'It's only for two weeks.'

She sighed. 'It's not that I don't want to, Hugh. It's...' Amy trailed off hopelessly. It was difficult to put into words exactly what were her objections.

Everything came so easily to Hugh. Exams, women, success in business, everything he wanted had always plopped on his plate as though some benevolent god were smiling on him. Any small hiccup in his plans had always been carefully smoothed and now it was her turn to be useful. *Good old Amy!* Except that 'good old Amy' didn't relish being suddenly noticed because she could be useful. Particularly today. Her birthday.

'Just two weeks,' he coaxed, watching her face closely. 'At least it will tide you over while there's nothing else in the pipeline—'

'How do you know that?' she cut across him, her eyes narrowing astutely. 'I suppose I don't need to ask where you got the impression I'd be grateful for anything. It can only have been Seb. I suppose that explains why it's all been left to the last minute.'

'He only said things were a bit quiet for you.'

'And how would he know?' she asked indignantly. 'He's not been down here for weeks. I've put in loads of applications to television companies. It might be very difficult for me to put my own life on hold.'

Seb pushed open the door with his bottom, perilously carrying three mugs of tea while ducking under the low cottage beam. 'But you will, won't you?' He smiled ingratiatingly across at Amy. 'You're the one with the flowers on it.'

'Sexist!' Amy retorted as she cleared the table of the Sunday newspapers and magazines.

Seb shrugged. 'Mum's taste in mugs, not mine, and if you will have sugar in your tea—take the consequences. How else do you expect me to remember which one's yours?' He handed a mug across to Hugh. 'Of course she'll do it.'

'Of course she won't! Not just like that.' She shot a look of pure dislike back at her favourite brother. 'I *want* to be a researcher, I *don't* want to be a secretary and even if I did I'd never choose to work for Hugh.'

'No, hideous prospect,' Seb agreed, flinging himself down in a leather club chair. 'Shouldn't care to do it myself, but think of your debts, little sister. Hugh's desperate. Name your price.'

Amy tucked a wayward strand of hair behind her ear and turned her attention back to Hugh. 'What kind of things does Sonya do?'

'Do?'

She nodded. 'Is she aggressive? Does she cry? If I agree I want to know the kind of things I'd have to protect you from.'

'It's nothing like that. She's calmly confident. Totally convinced there's a sexual attraction between us.'

'Even without encouragement?' she asked incredulously.

'She imagines there is. She's in no doubt I want her.'

'She's certainly persistent and becoming less subtle,' Seb cut in as he passed across a packet of biscuits. 'Tell her about Friday's package.'

'In the morning mail was a small parcel—' Hugh began

reluctantly, before stopping as the telephone rang from the depths of the hallway.

Seb grunted. 'Just when it's getting spicy. Hold the thought. I'll be back in a moment.'

'So?' Amy queried as the door closed gently behind him.

'She sent a packet of condoms, together with a hotel address, date and time.'

Amy, in the act of sipping, spluttered. 'I don't believe it.'

'Neither did Barbara.'

'That's so...so...tacky.'

'Isn't it?' Hugh agreed.

Seb opened the sitting-room door. 'Hugh, it's Callie. She wants a word.' Mutely he held the door open until Hugh obeyed the summons. Seb sat back down in the chair he'd vacated and picked up his mug. 'Did I miss much?'

'Nothing you don't know. I can't believe she sent Hugh a packet of condoms at work.'

'Variety condoms,' Seb added irrepressibly.

'Does that make a difference?'

'It does to Hugh's secretary. You haven't met her, but she is an absolute "spinster of this parish" type, probably never seen a condom in her life, let alone a variety pack. I know it's not funny, but I can't get rid of the picture of Barbara Shelton opening the parcel. Can you imagine any temp keeping something like that quiet? That's why I thought of you.'

Amy sighed as she felt the net tighten about her. It didn't matter how much she resented Seb's cavalier attitude to her time, he was right. She'd seen enough of the pain of marriage breakdown to last her a lifetime. Her mother had never really recovered from her father's leaving. The betrayal had scored in deep and left a wound that had festered until the day she'd died. If chaperoning Hugh would prevent her godfather being hurt, there was no way she could refuse.

'Poor Richard,' she said, watching the apricot roses softly bobbing at the window. It was so sad how everyone's lives went wrong. Richard had waited such a long time before deciding to marry, and then he'd gone and fallen for someone like Sonya. For someone whose business acumen was a byword in the City it was a strange anomaly he'd made such a poor choice in his personal life.

'Feel sorry for Hugh too. I know you don't like him much, but it's actually getting quite serious.'

She turned back to look at her brother. 'It's not that I don't like him.'

'Approve of him, then. He likes his women, but this isn't in the usual run of things. I know I'm trying to make light of it, but she'd be giving me the creeps. It doesn't matter what he says to her, she keeps coming on to him.'

'But—'

'There isn't any "buts". He needs someone to shield him until his PA gets back. It doesn't seem too much to ask. You know Mum would have forced you out the door if she was still alive.'

'It's not fair to use Mum,' she protested without much conviction, knowing her mother would have been among the first to volunteer the services of her daughter. She sighed and replaced her empty mug on the small table. 'I suppose I'm just finding it difficult to believe Hugh can't manage it all himself. I've watched him jettison women with a total disregard for their feelings since he turned about eighteen. Probably before that, but I was too young to notice.'

'Sonya's got the hide of a rhino. She's not even deterred by Callie and she's scary.'

'The woman on the phone?'

He nodded, pushing off his brogues with his toes and putting his socked feet up on the table. 'Calantha Rainford-Smythe. Hugh's latest. Money and connections oozing from every pore. Didn't you meet her at Christmas?'

It was difficult to forget a woman like Calantha. She was a tall streak of elegant blonde perfection who'd managed to see off any competition that evening by dint of clinging like a limpet. A typical Hugh appendage. 'I think so,' she said blandly, walking over to the piano. 'Jewellery designer, isn't she?'

His brown eyes crinkled. 'She likes to think so. In reality other people do the work and she puts her name to it.'

'What does she say about all this Sonya business?' she asked, drawing her finger along the dust on the piano lid.

'You can ask her yourself unless she's ringing to say she can't make it. She's supposed to be coming down.'

'I didn't know that,' Amy said, looking up.

'She was supposed to be in Brussels, but on balance Callie decided she couldn't miss Henley Royal Regatta. A great opportunity to see and be seen. Her business depends on it,' he said, mimicking her flat vowel sounds. 'All that champagne and old money about the place. Not to mention the risk that Hugh might meet someone else.'

Amy smiled. 'You don't like her, do you?'

'Not my type. I don't know what she thinks about Sonya, though. Hugh's never said. You'll have to ask him.'

'About what?' Hugh said, opening the sitting-room door.

'Callie's opinion of Sonya,' Seb said, lifting his feet off the table to let him pass. 'How did she know you were here?'

'She's just arrived at my mother's,' he said, sitting back

down on the sofa. 'I'll finish my tea and head back. I need to pick up my blazer and tie and I think Jasper and Ben are meeting us there as well. I don't know what time they planned on getting here.'

'What does she say about Sonya?'

There was a small beat before he answered. 'Callie doesn't know about Richard's health problems or really understand my relationship with him. Her perspective on it is therefore…different,' he said carefully.

'Meaning?'

Hugh's glance flicked across at Seb before he continued blandly, 'Meaning she thinks I should tell Richard what's going on. If the marriage is doomed there's no point prolonging it.' He picked up his mug and drained the last of the tea.

'Oh,' Amy said inanely into the silence. There was no compassion in that. No empathy. Richard had been foolish, but he didn't deserve to be so publicly humiliated by the people he loved. If—or rather when—the split came it would be so much better for it to have nothing to do with Hugh. 'Will Sonya and Richard drive over for the regatta?'

'Richard's not well enough this year. His angina has caused him a lot of discomfort recently—for all he doesn't want to admit it.'

'Are you going to do it, imp?' Seb asked, smiling at his sister's expression.

She chewed at her bottom lip. Her brother knew her too well. 'In theory…I suppose I could. But just for two weeks…and I'm going to charge you a ludicrous amount of money.'

'Excellent,' Seb said buoyantly. 'I knew you'd do it.'

'In theory. It's not as simple as you two make it sound. I don't think my overdraft is going to stretch to a bed and breakfast anywhere.'

'Who said anything about that? You can stay at my place,' Hugh said decisively as he stood up.

'I can't stay with you!'

'Of course you can. I've got plenty of room.'

Which rather missed the point she was trying to make. 'And Calantha? What will she think about that?'

Hugh frowned. 'Why should she think anything? It's the obvious thing to do. We can settle the final details later.' He turned to Seb. 'I do need to head back. Are you walking over to the house later?'

'Give us an hour. There's no desperate hurry. I drove the picnic over to the cricket pitch before any decent human being should be awake so we've bagged our spot.'

Amy let the conversation carry on without her as she slipped out of the door and up the narrow cottage stairs to her bedroom at the back of the house. Unobserved and unremarked upon, she thought, flopping on the black antique bed covered with the patchwork quilt her mum had finished the summer before she'd died.

Twenty-three today and unemployed—as Hugh had said. It was actually a bit depressing. Except not unemployed any longer. Somehow she'd agreed to become Hugh's PA and anything more degrading she could scarcely imagine. If he imagined for one moment she was going to make his tea and field telephone calls from would-be girlfriends, he was going to be disappointed.

But protect him from Sonya? Yes, she would do that.

She looked up at the crack in the low ceiling. And she'd have to stay in his home. There was no choice. The sofa bed in Seb's flat wasn't very appealing and her bank balance wouldn't stretch to the cost of commuting.

It would be nice to think Calantha wouldn't like it. It wasn't at all flattering for Hugh to be so completely unaware of her as a woman. She obviously hadn't registered on his antennae as anything other than 'little Amy, Seb's kid sister'. Which shouldn't bother her at all—but did. Obviously.

Jumping off the bed, she lifted the latch on the cupboard door where she kept her clothes and looked despairingly at the meagre contents. The cheque her father had sent for her birthday might have been used to buy something with 'wow' factor for the regatta, but it had arrived this morning and there hadn't been time.

The dress code was so specific: no trousers, no skirts with a split, not even the kind that wrapped around. The tiniest hint of a thigh had been known to cause apoplexy in the Stewards' Enclosure and would certainly result in being refused entrance. But then what did you expect when the rules had been created in the nineteenth century? All of which left her with no choice. The only dress she possessed that fell below the regulation knee length was a recent charity-shop buy in beige. It was pleasant, it was boring and it was as unremarkable as she was.

And who was she kidding? Hugh just had to sit there in his immaculately cut trousers and fix his deep blue eyes on her and she forgot he was shallow and arrogant with an appalling attitude to women.

Immune to Hugh? Of course she wasn't! Never had been.

She *should* be immune to him, *should* be completely inured to his sexy eyes and throaty laugh—but she wasn't. But at least she could make a fantastic job of making sure he didn't suspect it.

Amy threw the dress on the bed and swiped at the fly buzzing about the room before watching it bash itself against the small glass window-pane. That just about covered how she felt about herself. *Damn.*

CHAPTER TWO

CALANTHA RAINFORD-SMYTHE was everything she remembered.

Amy stood next to her, completely dwarfed and feeling
more sparrow-like than even she'd anticipated. There was
some small consolation in watching the difficulty Calantha
was having in preventing her spiky stiletto heels sinking
into the soft grass of the Champagne Lawn. It made her
grateful for her own flat pumps.

But there was no consolation to be found in the matter
of Calantha's soft coral dress. It fell to the regulation be-
low-knee length but the back looped so low you knew she
couldn't be wearing a bra and the silk fabric skimmed her
bottom so closely it suggested she couldn't be wearing
knickers either.

Amy sipped at her chilled fizzy alcohol and watched
Calantha's possessive hand, beautifully manicured, move
to rest gently on Hugh's cream blazer. She'd seen Hugh
with beautiful women so many times over the years, but
there was something about this one that really set her teeth
on edge. She was so self-assured. So perfect. So...unlike
her, she thought with a wave of inadequacy.

'Hugh and I went to the Maldives this February. We
had a simply marvellous time, didn't we, darling?' she said
with a turn of the head that set her earrings swinging,
drawing attention to a long and impossibly graceful neck.
'We stayed at Kanuhura, which is only about forty minutes
by seaplane from Male.'

It was obvious what Hugh saw in her. She was stunning

24

to look at. She probably looked great in a bikini on a beach in the Maldives, but Calantha was still a condescending snob with a sweet, sickly voice that personally made Amy feel nauseous.

'We stayed in a water villa. Totally fabulous. They're built on stilts with steps that lead directly into the water,' she continued, with an expressive wave of her manicured hand.

Amy looked away. Standing around eavesdropping on Calantha's conversation wasn't her idea of a great way to spend a birthday. Her eyes scanned the sky and watched ominous grey clouds blow across. They'd be lucky if the rain held off. She pulled her cardigan closer round her shoulders and wondered how Calantha could stand there looking elegant in practically nothing. The wretched woman didn't even seem to have a goose-pimple anywhere.

Looking back at her, she caught Hugh's eyes watching her. They twinkled engagingly as though it were a shared moment of amusement. Her mouth instinctively twitched as she felt his boredom radiate across the gap between them.

She allowed herself a small smile and gave half an ear to Calantha's eulogising about other perfect holiday destinations. Ben appeared to be enthralled and Jasper's girlfriend was gamely trying to outdo the blonde beauty in gushiness.

Seb touched her gently on the arm. 'When you've finished your drink, shall we go back to the car and set up the picnic? Ben wants to be back here by two to watch some friends row.'

'Do you need some help with that?' Hugh asked, cutting across Calantha.

'If you like,' Seb agreed. 'Amy's not much use lifting

out the hamper.' He took her empty glass out of her hand and passed it to Ben. 'Find somewhere to leave this. Give us half an hour and follow on. Same pitch as last year.'

Amy allowed herself to be propelled by a firm hand in the small of her back. Anything would be preferable to standing around listening to a boring conversation about places she couldn't afford to visit and people she'd never met.

Last year she'd quite enjoyed Henley Royal Regatta—but then last year Hugh hadn't been able to leave London. He'd been busy with a party of friends over from the States and had rung Seb to cancel. She'd quite enjoyed a day people-watching: handsome, athletic men wandering around and foolish ones drinking far too much. Ben, by virtue of now living in the quintessential English town of Henley, had become an associate member of the world-famous Leander Club and had taken them to tea. It had been pleasant.

This year, Hugh held court. When he was home everything always revolved around him and it irritated her. Even as she agreed to fall in with whatever he suggested it bothered her he should lead everyone so effortlessly. As soon as he said he was going to set up the picnic she could see the sparkle leave his girlfriend's conversation.

'Are you sure Calantha can spare you?' she asked pointedly as Hugh joined them.

His eyes gleamed with amusement, evidently aware of the waspish edge to her voice. 'I'm sure she'll manage,' he responded blandly.

'Did you ask if she wanted to be left with people she scarcely knows?'

'Do you think I should go back and ask her?'

Amy pulled her cardigan further onto her shoulders. 'Do what you like. It's none of my business.' She looked back towards the group, now rudderless. Calantha's long blonde hair blew in the breeze and the silk fabric outlined the shape of her legs. Into the silence she couldn't stop herself asking, 'How come she doesn't freeze in that dress? It's hardly a balmy summer day, is it?'

'It's cold, but women do that kind of thing.'

'But not our Amy,' Seb cut in, putting his arm around his sister.

'What do you mean?'

'You've dressed for comfort.'

'What's that supposed to mean?' she asked, shaking off his patronising arm.

'Nothing.'

'Just that I'm not dressed like Calantha.'

Seb looked surprised. 'Well, you're not, are you? I've never seen you wear anything like Callie chooses.'

Amy glanced down at her offending simple tunic dress with its demure circular neckline. If it had been made for a petite frame it would have been more flattering, but she was acutely aware how out of proportion it was on her. Certainly it would never be described as glamorous. She felt the sting of female pride behind her brown eyes and lifted her chin defiantly.

How *dared* Seb do this to her?

Unthinkingly cruel. She looked like what she was— someone who'd been eking out her existence on a student loan. What did Seb expect her to wear? He knew she'd had no financial help from their father at all with her degree. Being so much younger than him, she'd felt the full force of their father's bankruptcy whereas he'd been cosseted through his degree and launched on the London job market.

'Shut up, Seb. She looks fine.'

Hugh's intervention just made her feel worse. She sup-

posed he meant it kindly, but 'fine' was scarcely the way
she wanted to be thought of. She knew her tunic dress did
nothing for her figure. It flattened her breasts to practically
nothing and made her legs look too thin.

'She doesn't look fine,' Seb said with a searching look
at her. 'You know, Hugh, it's not going to work. This thing
about Amy going up to London with you. It's a great idea,
but it's not going to work unless we do something about
her clothes. If you think this dress is bad, you should see
the other things she wears.'

Both men turned to look at her as they walked and their
scrutiny wasn't flattering. If the floor could have opened
up and swallowed her she'd gladly have disappeared. Her
embarrassment, humiliation and total mortification were
paralysing. It was all the worse for being true. Seb's words
continued to whirl about her with a hateful accuracy.

'She can't go into an office dressed like that. I've never
seen any woman walk around Harpur-Laithwaite dressed
like that. And while we're at it she'd better do something
about her hair. She looks about sixteen.'

'She does look young,' Hugh agreed, looking thoughtful.

'You needn't talk about me as though I'm not here.'

'If she's going to be any kind of a match for Sonya, she
ought, at least, to look the part,' Seb continued relentlessly.
'Chief Executive's wife and all. She'll walk straight past
her.'

The pain in her chest was becoming uncomfortable as
she tried to keep up. She wasn't part of their conversation,
but since she was the subject of it she felt they should
show more consideration of her. 'Can you walk a little
slower?'

'Sorry,' Hugh said, immediately slackening his pace.
'We were just saying it's a pity you don't look older.'

Amy forced a smile to her face, but the hurt radiated from her. 'Can't do much about that.' She turned to look at Seb. 'You know perfectly well I don't have any money. What I do have is plenty of debts.'

He had the grace to look a little ashamed of himself. 'There's no need to get defensive, Amy. I'm only saying it like it is.'

'Are you?' she said dangerously.

Seb huffed. 'Well, it's true. You will need to power-dress for Harpur-Laithwaite. Hugh will have to buy you something to wear.'

'How kind of him. Do I get to choose my clothes myself or will they just arrive?'

Hugh's soft laugh only made her feel more irritated. This was personal. This *hurt*.

Seb laughed back at him and placed a heavy arm around her shoulders. 'Stop acting like a ruffled pigeon. It isn't like you to get moody.'

She shook him off. 'Only if I have extreme provocation. It might have something to do with the fact it's my birthday today and, please—' she held up a hand to stop him speaking '—don't even begin to tell me you forgot because I've already worked that out for myself.'

His expression was comical and the look of total horror on his face went some way to assuaging the cold, resentful feeling she'd had since breakfast. She heard the small, muttered expletive and saw the look of entreaty he cast at Hugh.

'Look, Amy, I'm sorry,' Seb began with a nervous laugh. 'I've got a hell of a memory.'

'Fine. But I think the least you can do is not annihilate me completely. I'm perfectly aware I've nothing to wear. Believe me, it's very boring dragging on the same pair of jeans each day and feeling grateful for the odd charity-shop find.' There was silence and Amy felt vaguely pleased at herself. 'Now, let's just set up this picnic and let the subject drop.'

She was aware of the closet glances passing between the two men, but she decided to ignore them. If they felt uncomfortable—good. She demanded very little of her brother, but his reminding her how unsuitably dressed she was for Henley's stylish regatta was a cut too much.

It wasn't as though she'd particularly wanted to go this year. It had been a casual assumption she'd join them and truthfully the alternative was worse. No one wanted to spend a birthday alone. She felt the hot prick of emotion behind her eyes and brushed away such foolish weakness with her hand.

Hell. This was embarrassing. *In front of Hugh.* She never cried. Certainly not over a lack of dresses or money. Just today she felt unbelievably lonely. One small, insignificant little boat cast adrift on a very big sea.

Hugh quietly passed her his handkerchief. She glanced up at him, surprised. His expression was soft and, for once, he wasn't smiling. 'Happy birthday.'

'It's not that. Not exactly. I'm just…well, I don't know. Missing Mum, I suppose.' It was true. Her birthday, her mum and Henley Regatta were all firmly entwined in her memory. When first Luke and then Seb had rowed here their mum had loved coming to watch them. Been so proud. Amy sniffed into the hanky. On certain days, on her birthday, the pain of being without her was still very raw.

Hugh didn't say anything. Instead he put his arm around her tense shoulders and pulled her into his hard, lean body. She could smell his distinctive aftershave and feel his comforting warmth. Just being held by him made her feel bet-

ter. Not small or insignificant any more. Nonsense, of
course. He was just being kind.

'Did anyone remember your birthday?' Hugh asked
softly as she relaxed into him.

She blew her nose in a small, defiant gesture. 'Of course.
I'm not completely unpopular.' She could feel his fingers
inadvertently touching her hair. He didn't know, didn't
have any idea of how being with him was making her feel.

'I wasn't suggesting—'

She rushed on. 'Some of my friends from uni sent me
cards. So did your mother, actually. She always sends a
card because it's the same day as your aunt Mary's in
Brighton.'

She could feel the sympathy emanating from him and
she didn't want that. It was galling to have him feel sorry
for her. She lifted her chin a little higher. 'And Dad and
Lynda sent me a cheque for my birthday.'

'Enough to clear your debts?'

Amy let her laughter bubble up. 'Hardly. Enough to buy
a few centimetres of the silk in your girlfriend's dress.
Richard bought me these,' she said, pushing back her hair
to show the twisted gold knots in her ears. 'They match
the necklace he gave me at Christmas.'

'They're beautiful.' And then, 'I'm sorry about your
birthday. We both are, aren't we, Seb?'

She shrugged. 'It doesn't matter.'

'It does. I can't believe I didn't remember,' Seb said
with real bemusement.

It was funny to watch him. Suddenly it didn't seem to
matter so much. With a half-laugh, half-sniff, she finally
tucked Hugh's handkerchief into her cardigan pocket. 'I'd
better wash this before I give it back to you.' She put her
hand out to catch Seb's. 'You never do remember. Not

since Mum died and there's been no one to remind you. Come on, let's get this picnic sorted.'

Picnic was scarcely the word to describe what she'd put together. By the time they'd assembled everything onto tables covered with starched linen tablecloths it looked more like something from a film about an Edwardian shooting party than anything twenty-first century.

'I can't believe I got you to do this on your birthday,' Seb remarked as he carried a large Brie to the table. 'Damn! I forgot the keys.'

'What?' she asked, taking it from him.

He didn't answer her, turning back to Hugh. 'The folding chairs are in the back of Jasper's Bristol. I'll have to walk back and get his keys. Stay and help Amy with the drinks.'

Amy calmly made more space on the table for the cheese. 'There's a crate of wine on the passenger seat,' she said, indicating back to Seb's MG, 'and that's it, really. We're done. Do you want to walk back and find Calantha?'

'I'll stay and talk to you,' Hugh said, carrying the crate out of the low-slung car and putting it down beneath the shade of the tree. 'They won't be long.'

'No.'

'Do you want a glass of wine now?'

'Why not?' she agreed, looking about her for somewhere to sit. There wasn't anywhere obvious. The ground was still very damp from the morning rain. She rummaged about in the boot to pull out the plastic sheeting Seb used to protect it. 'We'll have to sit on this until Seb gets back with the keys.'

Hugh picked up the corkscrew and carelessly lifted a bottle of white wine from the crate. His movements were so smooth and unconscious it looked as if he opened a bottle every day of his life. He probably did, Amy thought, spreading the sheet out. Not for him would there be little bits of cork floating in the wine.

She sat down with her back against the broad trunk of the horse-chestnut tree and shut her eyes against the image of Hugh.

'You look tired,' he remarked as he handed her a glass.

'I am.' Her fingers tingled at the slight contact of his.

Surely she'd outgrown this? She was *so* foolish to allow herself to be affected by Hugh Balfour. He had a girlfriend who could have been lifted from the pages of a magazine about to join them any minute. And that wasn't unusual. He always had some impossibly beautiful woman in his life. *It just wasn't going to happen.*

Men like Hugh Balfour went for long slithers of women who looked great in clothes and made other men envy them. Witness Calantha. They did *not*, she reminded herself forcefully, go for height-challenged women whom they'd known since before adolescence.

And that was just as well. She couldn't cope with Hugh. She wasn't resilient enough. 'Seb and I loaded up the car this morning at about five. I'm not used to those hours any more.'

'Were you ever?' he asked, sitting down beside her, his legs stretched out in front of him, his fingers curling casually around the stem of his glass.

'Just before Mum died she had problems sleeping. I got used to waking up when she did.' She sipped her wine, trying to ignore the way her stomach nervously twisted itself in knots just because he was there. 'It didn't seem to affect me then—how much sleep I had or didn't have—but I'm shattered today.'

'It's motivation,' he said, leaning his head back on the trunk. 'She was lucky to have you.'

Amy looked down self-consciously. 'I was lucky to have her,' she countered.

'Why can you never take a compliment?' Hugh asked, looking across at her curiously. 'Not many people would put their lives so completely on hold.'

'For their mum they would.'

'Seb and Luke didn't.'

'No.'

He took a sip of wine. 'Neither did your father.'

'He'd gone to Spain by then. When the business went bankrupt he didn't focus on anything much except that. And then he wouldn't have been able to cope with seeing Mum like…well, like she was at the end, even if they'd been together.'

Hugh reached out to brush a wavering strand of hair away from her hot face. 'And you could?' She looked away, obviously uncomfortable. Her blush spread in a mottled effect across her neck. *It was fascinating.* Other women couldn't cope with being ignored, but Amy was embarrassed by attention. 'For once in your life you'd better hear the truth about yourself. You were amazing to put off going to university to care for her. At eighteen. It was too much responsibility for someone so young.'

'I loved her,' she said simply.

'And that's all that matters?'

'Of course.'

She made it all sound so simple. She'd no idea how rare a quality she possessed. There'd never been a time when she hadn't put other people before herself. No wonder his mother adored her. 'Seb doesn't have any idea just what he has in you,' Hugh said with a smile before pulling himself to his feet. 'Do you want some more wine? It's your birthday, after all.'

She'd been about to refuse, but she allowed him to refill

her glass. The power of his words coursing through her veins was far more intoxicating than mere alcohol. The trouble with Hugh was, just when you thought you'd finally understood how shallow he really was, he was nice.

It was as if some shining god had suddenly turned round and noticed a lesser mortal. You. It kind of took your breath away for a moment—but then you had to remember this was *Hugh*. And he was a god with feet of clay.

'How come your father hasn't helped you out if you've got into debt?' he asked as he sat back down. 'He seems to be doing fairly well again now.'

She shrugged. 'He's under new management.'

'What's that got to do with anything?'

Her fingers picked at the grass. 'When Dad remarried, Lynda gently suggested they ought to concentrate their financial resources on building up the new business. She convinced him I'd be able to get a good job when I graduated and could use the government loan in the meantime.' His face remained blank and she managed a smile. 'It's not that bad. You don't need to pay it back until you're earning. Lots of students have them.'

'But not many people who have a parent as wealthy as yours,' he said dryly. 'Does Seb know about this?'

'Of course he does. There's nothing he can do about it. Or Luke either,' she said, thinking of her other brother.

'You don't seem angry about it.'

'I'm past that. It won't change anything, but Seb feels guilty.'

'I imagine he might. He was bailed out several times,' Hugh said, remembering two colourful incidents during their university career.

Amy smiled. 'Dad hadn't lost his money then. Seb knows it's pointless talking to him, but he still minds he can't help me himself. He's ploughing everything he can back into his own new business.'

'Yes, I know, but—'

'So even if he offered I wouldn't accept. It's not his problem.'

'What about Luke? He must be earning enough in medicine.'

Amy shook her head at the thought of her other brother helping financially. 'He's practically working for just board and lodging at the moment. He's employed by a charity and based at a remote hospital in Africa.'

'I didn't know.'

She looked up at him. 'Didn't you? He flew out eighteen months ago.'

'Not about Luke. About you. I'd no idea Lynda was like that.'

'Don't say it like that. She's not a bad person. She's just not used to the concept of family. She's an only child herself, never been married before, never had any children of her own, and at forty-seven it all came as a bit of a shock to her. Besides, it's not just her. Dad doesn't like parting with money any more than she does. Not now. Not after the bankruptcy. He's irritated we got Mum's cottage.' She smiled up at him. 'It's not your problem.'

'It ought to be Seb's. Can't he speak to your dad?'

'I'd rather he didn't. Besides, Luke, Seb and I do own the cottage. It was always kept in Mum's name so it didn't go with everything else and she left it to us. When we sell it I can clear all my debts, but none of us want to put it on the market just yet.'

'Why? Seb could do with an injection of cash and so could you.'

'It'll take time to sell and until I find myself a job I don't have the money to rent a flat.'

'Ah.'

'It'll work out. Hopefully I'll find something while I'm staying with you. I hope I won't let you down,' she said, deliberately changing the subject. 'I've only done the odd temp job, you know?'

'Keep me out of Sonya's clutches and I won't complain.'

'Even if I wipe a vital document off your computer system?'

He smiled, wicked laughter in the depths of his blue eyes. She felt her stomach twist over at the blatant sexiness of it. Irresistible. He was irresistible—*almost*.

She just had to keep reminding herself of his track record with women. One at a time, one after another. A serial monogamist who never risked allowing anyone close enough to touch the core of him.

'Then I'll kill you,' he whispered softly, and she smiled as he'd intended she should.

'I'm scared. Tell me about Harpur-Laithwaite. Is it all carpet pile and pot plants? What kind of things do the women wear?'

'I don't know.'

'Don't believe you haven't noticed, Hugh,' Amy teased, and chuckled at the look he threw her. 'You're going to have to be a bit more helpful than that. Is it a jeans-and-casual-top sort of place or smart suits?'

She knew Harpur-Laithwaite was an investment bank and that Hugh advised traders on what to trade on, but it was scarcely a lot to go on.

He rested his head back on the tree trunk. 'Somewhere in between smart and casual. Barbara, my PA, wears a jacket, but you don't have to.'

'Good. I don't have one.'

'Not at the moment, maybe, but we're going to have to do something about your clothes. Seb's right about that.'

'You can't buy my clothes.'

'Of course I can. If I'm asking you to play the part of my PA, it's my responsibility to kit you out appropriately. Just try and buy something that reflects my importance and social standing.' He glinted.

'I can't—'

'You don't have a choice since you're cash-poor. If you feel an attack of scruples just remind yourself you're doing me a favour and I'm grateful.'

She looked at him with wide eyes, knowing she ought to refuse, but the temptation was just too great. 'How much…how much do you want me to spend?'

He scarcely gave it a thought before stating a figure that made her head swim. She hadn't had anything to spend on clothes for the past seven years and suddenly it felt as if she'd entered fairy-tale land. 'Buy what you need.'

'I won't need all that.'

'Then buy something for fun.'

'What are you trying to do? I feel like you're playing Fairy Godmother to my Cinderella.' She laughed in an attempt to cover her embarrassment.

He leant over and kissed her cheek. 'Godfather. Take it as a birthday present. Just make sure you take care in picking Prince Charming.'

As if there were any difficulty about it at this moment—given the choice. 'Promise,' she whispered, feeling the imprint of his lips where they'd touched her cheek.

With a feeling of unreality she watched as the others began to walk towards them. The short birthday idyll was over and she was back to the tedium of reality. She fixed a bright smile to her face as Jasper came towards her.

'Seb's just told us,' he said, pulling her to her feet. 'Happy birthday.'

But when he kissed her cheek it didn't work the same magic.

CHAPTER THREE

AMY was quietly pleased. Two wolf whistles and one improper suggestion and she'd only been in London for a couple of hours. But then that was London's tube network for you. That, plus a great haircut and some new clothes. This kind of feeling could become addictive. It didn't matter that the weather was humid and the heat was bouncing back off the city pavements.

She crossed the road and peered at the piece of paper in her hand. This was it. Hugh's house. She was no expert but the façade looked to be Georgian with a grand, symmetrical arrangement of windows. It was gorgeous. Hugh could have looked like the back end of a bus and you'd be tempted for a place like this.

Fitting the key in the lock, she felt a vague sense of surprise when the door opened. This really *was* going to be her home for the next couple of weeks. The inner sanctum of the spider's lair. *Amazing.* 'Hugh? Hugh, are you here?' she called tentatively into the echoey silence of a cavernous hall.

There was no answer. Amy pulled her bag into the hallway and closed the door behind her. 'Hugh?'

Still silence, except for the sound of her heels on the hardwood floor. Gingerly she pushed open the door immediately to her left and took in the muted colours and antique furniture. She let out a low whistle. *Classy.* It put his mother's words into a whole new perspective.

'I do hope he'll look after you properly, Amy,' she'd said the previous afternoon over a cup of tea and some

home-made cupcakes. 'He lives in a strange old place right
near a busy road and he's scarcely got a stick of furniture.
Nothing to make it homely.'

Amy smiled gently to herself. Hugh's mother would
hate this restrained elegance, with every piece of furniture
chosen to make an impact. Not a floral Austrian blind in
sight. It was simply a million miles away from his
mother's taste for frilly, soft furnishings and accumulation
of clutter. She quietly shut the door behind her.

He'd told her she'd find her room 'up the stairs and the
first door on the left'. Picking up her bag, she followed
his instructions and found a note stuck on the door. 'Hi.
I've put some towels on the bed. Help yourself to the wine
in the fridge,' she read, smiling as she pulled the note off
the creamy-white woodwork. Trust Hugh to think of wine
when any sensible woman would be dying for a cup of
tea.

Her room was light and fresh with a feel of *Pride and
Prejudice* about it and, as he'd said, fresh towels were
temptingly piled on the bed. It was just fantastic. Nothing
like she'd imagined. She thought he'd have gone for a
modernistic bachelor pad but this was totally 'Hugh' too.
The antique furniture gleamed and smelt of beeswax.
Compared with the house she had shared while at university, this was pure fantasy land. In fact everything about
the whole situation was like something lifted out of a
novel.

Amy shook her hair in the mirror, still fascinated by the
way it framed her face and made her eyes suddenly appear
enormous. Maybe the scissor-wielding genius was right
and her eyes were her best feature. At any rate he'd
squeezed her in on a Saturday morning and had done all
he'd promised and more.

What would Hugh make of her new image? It would be

nice to think he'd take one look at her and be staggered
by her transformation. Perhaps he'd even fall at her feet
and swear undying love on account of her beauty.

Of course, if he did that would make him very shallow.
She plonked down her bag and grabbed one of the white
towels before heading towards the *en suite*. But then he
was shallow, wasn't he? Even so, it wasn't likely she was
going to suddenly become the object of his desire. Which
was *good*, she reminded herself.

Anyway, Hugh didn't swear undying love. It wasn't in
his make-up. The best he'd ever offer would be an affair
for as long as it felt good. Getting involved with Hugh
would be like hitting a self-destruct button. And she wasn't
that stupid.

But she *was* in London. She *did* have new clothes. Life
was going to get better, she thought buoyantly, before
needing to concentrate on how Hugh's up-to-the-minute
design-statement shower head actually worked.

Later, fantastically cool with wet hair bundled up turban
style in a towel, she padded back to the bedroom to answer
the persistent bleep of her mobile. 'Hello.'

'Amy?'

'Yep.' She sat down on the edge of the bed feeling
strangely breathless, as if she'd been caught somewhere
she'd no right to be. It was so strange being in Hugh's
house. Touching his things.

'You sound guilty. What are you up to?' Hugh's warm
voice teased. 'Are you on your way?'

'No, I'm here.' She heard her voice quaver and bit her
lip. 'Just had a shower to cool off and am dripping on your
rug.'

'You managed the tube okay?'

Amy curled up more comfortably on the bed. 'I'm not
a complete country bumpkin. I did experience momentary

panic when the ticket thing ate my card, but it spat it out straight after. On the whole I managed fine.'

'Have you found everything you need?' he asked, and she could hear the smile in his voice.

'Yep. I love your house. It's gorgeous.'

He laughed. 'Make yourself at home. I should be back in about twenty minutes. Maybe less.'

'Twenty minutes?' She looked down at her towel-wrapped body.

'Put the kettle on,' he said just before the soft click ended the connection.

Twenty minutes.

Twenty minutes was no time at all. Impossible to even attempt putting back together the transformed image she'd arrived with. The lady in the shop had been very encouraging, but she doubted the aubergine eyeliner was as easy to apply as she'd made it sound.

With a sense of urgency she pulled on a pair of jeans and a simple T-shirt. There was no time to find a hair-dryer so she made do with twisting her hair out of the way and holding it in place with a plastic clip. It was scarcely the fairy-tale transformation she'd played out in her imagination, but maybe this was better. Just play it cool.

Bare-footed, she ventured downstairs in plenty of time to be waiting to meet him as he opened the front door.

'Did you have a good day at the office, darling? You really shouldn't be working on a Sunday you know.'

Hugh's face crinkled with amusement. 'It was important. Hell, it's hot out there,' he said, loosening his tie. 'What time did you arrive?'

'About three,' she said, offering a cheek for him to kiss. Dressed in a sharp city suit, he looked like a stranger, but the scent of his aftershave was reassuringly Hugh. 'It was easy to find. I walked around with my *A-Z* like a tourist and managed beautifully.'

He laughed. 'Have you had time for a drink?'

'Not yet.'

'Come on,' he said, leading her down the corridor, pausing only to throw his jacket over the banister rail, 'I need something now. My throat's parched.'

The kitchen was square with a slate floor and pale maple units. 'I love the granite,' she said, running her finger along the cold worktop. 'Very nice.'

Hugh looked in the fridge. 'What do you want? Fresh orange? Tea? Coffee?' he asked, turning to look at her. She had her hands pushed down into her jeans' back pockets and the pale pink T-shirt pulled tight across a bra-less chest, nipples clearly showing through the fabric. Unbelievably he felt a sudden urge to rub his thumb across each protruding nub. Wondered what it would feel like to let his hand wander up beneath her top and feel the soft, shower-cooled skin beneath.

'Orange, I think.'

'Right,' he said, turning back to the fridge. Stunned. This was *Amy*. What was he thinking of?

He poured the orange into a glass and handed it across, but he hadn't been mistaken. Beneath the baggy, shapeless clothes he'd always seen her in was something infinitely more interesting. His eyes helplessly returned to those nipples. He felt like some adolescent schoolboy suddenly caught looking at something he had no right to. 'Do you want to find some shade in the garden?'

'Whatever.'

He poured himself a glass of orange and turned to open the doors into the garden. 'There's some shade at the end.'

Amy peered curiously out. It was a small town garden but had obviously been designed in such a way as to give distinct areas. In the far corner there was a seat beneath a pergola dripping with clematis. 'Are you coming?' she asked, looking back at him.

'Lead the way.'

Inevitably his eyes followed the way her hips swung, followed the firm, rounded curve of her buttocks. Something about the heat must be getting to him. Amy was almost an honorary kid sister. It felt like a betrayal to be thinking about her in this way—particularly when she was only here to do him a favour. He sat down on the wooden seat and shifted uncomfortably. 'Have you bought yourself any clothes yet?'

'Can't you tell? This T-shirt is new.'

The pride in her voice only made him feel worse. 'It's great.' It was more than great. It was a simple T-shirt and it was single-handedly changing all his preconceptions about her.

'I may have overspent, Hugh,' she said, sipping her orange. 'I was doing fine until I caught sight of a suede suit I had to have. If it's too much I'll pay you for it once I'm paid, but don't make me take it back.'

He laughed and forced his equilibrium to settle. 'I don't think that's likely. A few outfits aren't going to ruin me and I'm too grateful you're here to complain.'

'How grateful?' she asked over the rim of her tumbler. 'There were some shoes...'

'Witch! I never had you down as a clothes woman.'

'Never had the opportunity.'

'I still don't get that,' he said, forcing his mind back to something he could genuinely feel disgust about. 'Surely your dad doesn't keep you as short of money as all that? Not now.'

'He doesn't see it like that. He sees it as "making my own way".' He went to speak, but she forestalled him.

'Leave it, Hugh. Let's talk about something else.' She drained the last of her orange. 'I hope I don't let you down. I'm a bit nervous about tomorrow.'

'There's no need to be.'

'I know you, Hugh. You'll go ballistic at the first mistake I make.'

'I don't do that.'

'Not to other people, perhaps, but to me you will. You always have.'

Laughter immediately lit his face and Amy reverted to the person he remembered. 'Unfair. If you're referring to your efforts to type my PhD you deserved my wrath. You were hopeless. I could have done it quicker with two fingers.' He took her glass out of her hand and replaced it with his own. 'Stop complaining and drink this.'

'But it's yours.'

'I've got nothing contagious I know about. I'd rather have a beer.'

She followed him back to the kitchen. 'Hugh?' He turned round. 'What's happened with Sonya this week? Anything?'

He poured his beer into a tall glass and waited for the froth to settle before he answered. 'One other package. A follow-up to the previous Friday's—'

'Condoms,' she said for him.

'Exactly. The worst development is Richard deciding he wants to hold his retirement party at their home. I can't not go, obviously, but Sonya on her own territory is worrying. I was hoping he'd pick a more neutral place.'

Amy put her glass down on the kitchen worktop and repositioned the clip in her hair, sublimely oblivious to the way her T-shirt pulled tight across her chest. His eyes instinctively took in the gentle swell of each pert mound.

The thought of her naked beneath that top was beginning to cause him serious trouble.

'She'll hardly do anything if her husband's there. Won't you be taking Calantha to it anyway? She should be able to get you home in one piece.'

'Yes.'

'You don't sound too sure.'

'I'll take Callie to the party,' he said with more conviction. Now wasn't the moment for trading in a girlfriend, however suffocating she might be becoming. It had started as a perfectly pleasant affair, both wanting the same things and knowing the rules. But now the balance was shifting. Callie wanted marriage. She wanted commitment and children. Not unreasonable, but not on offer with him. It never had been. He didn't want that kind of complication in his life.

Amy continued, blithely unaware of his train of thought. 'You've got me in the office, Calantha to hang off your arm socially. I think you're fairly safe.'

'Maybe.'

'Are you expecting anyone?' she asked as the doorbell rang.

'Not that I know of.' He put down his beer and started for the door.

'Hugh, what was in Sonya's last package?'

'Purple mesh panties.'

Amy opened her eyes wide. 'For you?'

He paused in the doorway and his lopsided grin flashed. 'That thought hadn't occurred to me. I'd better get the door.'

'Whoever's there is coming anyway,' Amy remarked at the sound of a key turning in the lock.

'Darling?' *Unmistakably Calantha.*

At the one word all Amy's happy, buoyant optimism

evaporated. Naturally Calantha would have a key to Hugh's house. Free to come and go as she pleased. Amy could feel her body tense at the thought of how in the way she was here. For a short while Hugh had made her feel a welcome guest. Someone he'd invited purely for the pleasure of her company.

She mustn't allow herself to forget why she was really here. The only way she was going to survive being in Hugh's company for the next two weeks was to remember. It wouldn't hurt, either, to remember the way Hugh operated. Carelessly sexy, moving on when boredom struck, as it inevitably did.

Honestly compelled her to admit that Calantha looked incredible. She was dressed in a sharply sexy dress, deep navy with a split up to her mid-thigh. Amy felt as though she had become monochrome, fading into the background. You couldn't compare a stick-thin, sophisticated woman with perfect bone structure and legs that stretched to heaven with someone who looked sixteen and had stopped growing at five feet two.

Calantha stopped and made a graceful turn, showing enough of her cellulite-free thigh to presumably send Hugh's blood pressure up into the stratosphere. 'Hello. Amy, isn't it?'

Amy nodded.

The blonde's blue eyes made a cursory sweep of her and obviously found nothing too much to worry about because her smile broadened. Irritated, Amy lifted her chin slightly. Whatever the other woman might think, she wasn't in the running for Hugh's attention. She knew far, far too much about him. There was no way she could cope with the knowledge that some day, some time, he'd move on.

As all men seemed to.

Calantha moved over to Hugh and pressed a proprietorial kiss against his lips. It was the mark of ownership and Amy felt her insides churn. 'Hello, darling. Sorry to make you come to the door. I thought I'd left my key at home.'

Hugh moved back slightly. 'Do you want something cool to drink? Amy and I were just talking in the garden.'

'I could join you for a few minutes but I need to get ready for tonight. That's why I'm here. Just checking you haven't forgotten.' Her lips curved into a smile, but no warmth reached her eyes. There was absolutely no softness there, merely a calculating, cold assessment of whether or not Amy was competition. 'We have a charity dinner this evening. Hugh has the most appalling memory for what he doesn't want to do.'

Amy smiled. 'That explains what he has in common with my brother.'

'Of course. Forgetting your birthday. Unforgivable.' Calantha turned as Hugh pressed a cool orange juice in her hand. 'Thank you. Are we going out into the garden?'

She led the way out through the French doors. 'I love this garden of Hugh's. I was thinking we ought to think about adding some honeysuckle to the rose arch. The scent would be lovely.'

Amy got the message. Loud and clear. Hugh was out of bounds. She supposed it was something of a compliment for Calantha to think she might hold any temptation for him. Something about her well-fitting jeans and trendy T-shirt perhaps? No one had ever thought it a possibility before. Of course, it might be simply that Hugh's girlfriend was feeling particularly vulnerable at the moment. That was more likely.

'What do you think?' Calantha asked, suddenly turning to her.

'Er…' she said, looking towards the rose arch. 'I suppose it's up to Hugh.'

Calantha's laugh tinkled musically. 'Trust me, I'm a designer.' She laid a beautiful hand on Hugh's knee. 'Had you remembered about tonight?'

Hugh's face was strangely shuttered, which told Amy Calantha's days were probably numbered. This was not Hugh hungry for the chase. If the other woman sensed his apathy it explained her antagonism to Amy.

'I told you I'd pick you up at eight.'

'I just wondered, with Amy's arrival, whether it might have slipped your mind?' she purred.

'No.'

Amy actually felt compassion for Calantha. How would it feel to have been so close to him and then have him end it? He always did it so abruptly and without a backward glance.

Calantha turned to look at her. 'It's such a shame on your first night in London, but these tickets are like gold dust. Everyone will be there. Chrissie Langerford and Flinty Rommer have agreed to wear some of my jewellery. With Flinty I almost can't fail to make the newspapers somewhere.' Calantha crossed her legs and the skirt fell open, displaying a huge length of thigh. 'They're models,' she explained.

'I know.'

'Impossible for Amy not to have done,' Hugh said dryly.

Calantha's fingers massaged his muscular thigh. 'That's what makes it so exciting for me. I was sure you wouldn't mind being left to your own devices for the evening. Hugh thought it a little unfair on your first night in London.'

'I'll manage.'

'That's what I said. I knew you'd be bound to have friends somewhere.'

Finally Amy felt her ire begin to rise. Compassion only went so far. There was no reason for Calantha to take Hugh's lack of interest out on her. She kept her voice steady. 'Actually I'd rather just settle in here. I'm a little nervous about tomorrow.'

'I forgot. It's your first job.' Calantha looked at her with such sympathetic understanding. 'I'm sure this will help you find a permanent job. It's a good opportunity for you to get some real work experience behind you.'

'I can't believe Hugh's given me the opportunity,' she replied dryly, and was rewarded with a crack of laughter from her new boss.

'She's doing me the favour, Callie. Against her better judgement, so don't push her too far.' Hugh smiled across at her and the ill feeling disappeared. His smile really did work magic. It was in his eyes and the narrow indentation in his cheek.

'You're welcome.'

His smile deepened.

Calantha observed it and her eyes narrowed as she turned back to Amy. 'I'm sure I recognise you. From before last weekend, I mean?'

'We met at Christmas.'

'At my mother's party,' Hugh confirmed.

Calantha's eyelids fluttered down to conceal her expression. 'I remember. Yes. You dropped a tray of mince pies.'

'Story of my life.'

'So embarrassing for you. Weren't you with a boyfriend? Graeme something, wasn't it?'

'Gregory.'

'That's it, Gregory. A nice boy, I thought.'

Which just about put him in his place, Amy thought. Gregory Hinchman had not been a nice boy at all.

'Are you still seeing him?'

'No.' She forced a smile. 'Not for a few months.'

'What a pity. I'm sure you'll find someone else.'

'Possibly.' Amy stood up. This was one conversation she was not prepared to have with the blonde stick insect. And certainly not in front of Hugh. Besides, it was none of Calantha's business and she was only asking because she wanted to hurt her. 'Look, I'll leave you two to make your arrangements. I've not had time to unpack yet.'

Hugh stood up with her. 'There aren't any to make. Callie needs to get back home and get ready. I'll pick you up at eight as arranged.'

It was to her credit, Amy thought, that the painted mouth didn't falter. Calantha continued smiling. 'Marvellous.' She gracefully unwound herself from the wooden bench. 'I'm so glad to have finally placed you, Amy. I was certain we'd met before Henley, but I just couldn't put my finger on when,' she said before sashaying back to the house with Hugh. 'Don't forget, darling, eight o'clock.'

Amy heard Hugh say something in his deep voice, but it was impossible to distinguish what. And none of her business either, she reminded herself as she picked up the discarded glasses. She fancied there'd been a trace of disapproval in the usually laughing blue eyes, as though he had been aware of the barbs his girlfriend had sent in her direction. But then that was probably fanciful thinking. Men were notoriously bad at picking up the signals passing between women.

She pulled a wry face. As bad as women were at sensing what was going on in the minds of men. If Amy was reading the signs correctly, Calantha was on her way out. She obviously felt vulnerable but Amy doubted she knew how close the axe was to falling. Or maybe she did. Maybe that was why she was being so catty.

Hugh was a difficult man to be involved with. Amy had

seen it all before. Knew what that glitter of boredom in his blue eyes meant and had seen his cruelty. She remembered Emma Lawson sitting on the wall outside her house ten summers ago and sobbing as though the world had ended. From that moment on, Amy had known how dangerous Hugh was.

Not that it was her business. Not then, not now. She opened the French doors into the kitchen as he was coming in from the hall.

'You didn't need to do that,' Hugh said, indicating the glasses.

'Pick them up? It's not that much effort.' She put them down on the side. 'Do these go in the dishwasher?'

She could feel his eyes continue to watch her. 'I put everything in there. Amy…I'm sorry about tonight.'

'It's not a problem.'

'If I could get out of it, I would.'

She turned to face him, her fingers resting on the worktop and the cold granite pressing into her palms. 'Why should you? You'll have more than enough of my company over the next two weeks. Don't worry about it.'

But he did worry about it. There was something about the thought of Amy left alone on her first night in London that really bothered him. His fingers closed around the stem of his wineglass and he swirled the blood-red liquid thoughtfully, watching the way the light played on the dark colour.

He'd known this was coming. Had recognised the signs of mind-numbing boredom whenever Callie spoke, but it was bloody poor timing. Richard's retirement party was under a week away and he needed her as a shield. And yet the prospect of keeping up the pretence, of taking Callie back to her flat and spending the night, did nothing for him.

He responded absent-mindedly to a remark by a middle-aged lady to his left and reviewed his options. He could carry on as he'd been doing for the past month or he could finish his relationship cleanly. He sat back in his chair.

Amy slept, curled cat-like in the depths of an armchair. She looked so innocent. Her hair still in that ridiculous plastic clip and her face completely clear of make-up. She was actually very lovely, fresh and clean and wholesome.

'Amy,' he said softly, touching her arm. 'Wake up. It's late. It's time you were in bed.'

She stirred slightly. The only sign she'd heard him was a faint fluttering of the dark eyelashes resting on her pale cheeks. 'Amy...'

This time she mumbled and tried to turn over. Sleepy brown eyes looked up into his face. 'Hugh,' she said, with a soft smile lighting up her face. 'You're back.'

And he wanted to kiss her.

What was happening to him? He'd known Amy for years and never felt the slightest inclination to do anything of the sort. He'd picked her up when she'd fallen off her horse and broken her wrist at fourteen without the slightest stirring of the emotions troubling him now. Even when he'd held her while she'd sobbed at her mother's funeral he hadn't felt the stirrings of any attraction. This was *Amy*.

It was like being in the room with a stranger. He'd never before noticed the faint blue veins in her tiny wrists or the golden threads in her brown eyes. He could feel the sudden, inexplicable stirring of desire. He moved away from the seat, putting distance between them, feeling ashamed of himself.

He threw his jacket over the back of the sofa. It had to be some kind of reaction to leaving Calantha at the door to her flat. It was unprecedented. He always went in, stayed until the early hours and then drove home. He could still see her amazed expression as soon as she'd realised he'd had no intention of following her inside.

'It's Amy, isn't it?' she coaxed. 'Don't be such a fool. She won't expect you back tonight. She's a big girl.' But he gently took her hands away from his shoulders and made some spurious excuse about being tired.

'Phone me,' she called after him. He'd have to but he didn't want to. This wasn't a time in his life when it would be wise to be between girlfriends.

He turned back to look at Amy and caught her struggling to sit up, still heavy with sleep. 'I'm sorry to have woken you, but I couldn't let you stay there like that. You'd end up with a very stiff neck.'

She pulled her dressing-gown closer about her. It was a heavy white towelling robe, old and very unattractive. It was also too short on the sleeves and pulled tight across her chest. It should have had the effect of a cold shower, but somehow it didn't. He wondered how long she'd owned it. Whether it was yet another symptom of having no money to spend on clothes. She was answering him and he struggled to bring himself back to concentrate on what she was saying.

'I didn't mean to. I'm just so tired. What time is it?'

'Eleven.'

'Eleven? Is that all? I didn't expect you back so early.'

He moved over to a side-table and poured himself a large whisky from the decanter. 'Do you want anything?' he asked over his shoulder.

'No, thanks.'

He felt better with a whisky glass cradled between his hands. His fingers felt the indentations in the cut glass and he let the burning liquid fire his throat before sitting on the sofa.

'Bad evening?' Amy asked, tucking her feet underneath her and yet again readjusting that old dressing-gown.

He saw her do it and watched her eyes check her body for any gaping flesh. He wanted to know whether she was naked under there. What would happen if he went across and opened the belt at her tiny waist and looked? He really wanted to look.

Hugh took another quick gulp of whisky. He was going out of his mind. 'I suppose it was a bad evening.' He drained the last of the liquid and set the empty glass down on the table. Suddenly two weeks seemed like a very long time.

CHAPTER FOUR

TOMORROW, in Amy's opinion, came all too soon. As she resisted the temptation to roll back over and carrying on sleeping she felt a small knot of apprehension settle in her tummy. This whole idea of being Hugh's secretary was a terrible mistake. She should never have agreed to it.

Besides, it was far too early to begin a day, she thought as she reached for her dressing-gown and then leant over the side of the bed to search for her slippers. She swore softly as the left one eluded her grasp and then made a determined grab at it. Emerging triumphant, she sleepily stuffed her arms into her towelling dressing-gown and headed for the *en suite* bathroom.

Switching on the mirror light, Amy peered at her reflection with dissatisfaction. She looked like a teenager, she thought disgustedly. Sonya Laithwaite wasn't going to take her seriously looking like this. She was going to be a terrible secretary and, in all probability, fail to protect Hugh from Sonya. Richard would discover just what kind of woman his wife really was. He'd have a heart attack and die—and it would all be her fault!

But it was too late to back out now. Much too late. She was committed, as much from the inordinate amount she'd spent on clothes as from her desire to protect her godfather from the kind of heartache her mother had suffered.

'Breakfast in fifteen minutes,' Hugh shouted through the door, making her jump nervously. 'I've left you a cup of tea on the side-table.'

Amy wrenched open the door and stuck her head round the side. 'You could have killed me then!'

'What do you want for breakfast?'

'Just toast and strong coffee,' Amy replied, pulling her head quickly back inside, making a mental note to avoid catching sight of Hugh immediately before or after he took a shower. There was something very unnerving about seeing a partially clothed Hugh Balfour.

He was *gorgeous*.

But then she'd always known that. However, it was one thing to know it theoretically, it was quite another to have it displayed so obviously in her bedroom. Amy scrubbed at her face with her flannel. The image of small dark hairs curling on his chest, and muscular biceps that proved he'd no need to feel guilty about missing the gym this morning, was going to be difficult to erase.

She stomped back into the bedroom. She had to get herself under control. It wasn't that she was really attracted to Hugh, she told herself for the umpteenth time. That would be an impossibility, she thought as she ferreted about for her new bra and knickers in the bottom of her suitcase. Hugh would never be the type of man she'd consider. Only stupid women wanted to be part of a continuous procession of bedfellows. And *she* wasn't stupid.

Sonya had to be the strangest woman on the planet. Why would she risk her comfortable and wealthy position as Richard's wife for a meaningless fling with Hugh? There weren't biceps developed that would tempt Amy to behave in such a foolish way. But then other women hadn't had the benefit of living so close to someone else's heartache. Her father's uncontrollable lapses had peppered their lives with sadness. Why did people have to be so cruel to other people? Particularly when they'd promised to love them? She didn't understand it.

Amy slipped into her underwear, pausing for a sip of tea before choosing a fitted red skirt and black T-shirt. Of course women had fallen over themselves to share Hugh's bed, on whatever terms he'd cared to dictate, ever since she could remember. But why? They had to know it wouldn't last. She took another swig of tea before starting on her make-up.

Hugh rapped on the door. 'Coffee is on the side. I'll be down again in a couple of minutes.'

'Okay.' Amy sat back in her seat and pouted at her reflection. It was actually quite good. From somewhere she seemed to have magically created cheekbones and her eyes had grown in size.

Best of all was the suggestion of a cleavage. She stood up and admired herself in the full-length mirror by the window. The bra, clearly worth the ridiculous amount of money she'd paid for it, had brought about a miracle. For the first time in her life she appeared to have a bust. It might not rival anything Sonya Laithwaite could boast of, but at least it had been arrived at without the use of silicone.

Pausing to slip on high-heeled black shoes and pick up her sexy little red handbag, she closed the door to her room. 'Do you want me to pour you a coffee?' she called at the muffled sounds coming from his room down the corridor.

'Thanks. Black, no sugar,' he replied through the closed door.

Amy walked down the stairs feeling more buoyant about the day than she would ever have expected. There was something marvellous about new clothes. She only hoped Hugh would think she looked all right to fit into his office. At the very least she looked older and, she hoped, more capable.

She poured herself a mug of coffee and looked around for some sugar. The first cupboard she opened was completely empty, the second had a meagre selection of tins and a bag of opened sugar. Amy pulled open the nearest drawer and found the spoons. 'Don't you ever eat at home?' she asked as the kitchen door opened.

'Not often. I prefer to eat out,' he replied, appearing from beneath a towel, his dark hair tousled and wet, his chest still bare.

Amy looked away and hurriedly opened one of the lower cupboards. *Why didn't the wretched man put on some clothes?*

What Hugh noticed first was the way the fabric of her skirt moulded itself around a small, pert behind. He found the words he'd been about to say dry in his throat as he discovered just what Amy had been hiding beneath those jeans.

And it couldn't have come at a worse time.

Amy had legs. Shapely legs encased in fine black stockings—or perhaps they weren't stockings, but his imagination was working overtime. He'd always thought of her as small when, in fact, she was petite, finely boned and bloody, bloody sexy. He stood mesmerised, foolishly standing clutching the damp towel to his body.

She swivelled round. 'What do you think? Will I do?'

He put the towel down on the work surface. 'Did I buy all that?'

'You'd better. I've spent a fortune. It's part of our deal.'

Hugh walked across the kitchen and took a strand of her bobbed hair between his fingers. 'I didn't notice your hair last night.' He found it difficult to concentrate on what he'd meant to say as her brown eyes looked up at him. He'd never really noticed them before—not in this way. 'You...you look lovely.'

'But do I look older?'

Hugh let his hand drop to his side. *Yes. She looked older.* His eyes took in the shadowy cleft between her breasts, the way her neck stretched elegantly and her hair danced. He deserved to be shot for the thoughts he was thinking. *About Amy!*

And that was the point. Amy was the kid sister of his best friend and Seb would undoubtedly do the shooting if he took these thoughts any further.

'Not many women would want to hear their clothes aged them,' he said lightly, turning away to pick up his towel.

'You know what I mean. Do I still look sixteen? I want to look the part.'

He swung the towel across his right shoulder, an unreadable expression in his blue eyes. 'You look fantastic. Has Seb seen you dressed like that?'

'No.'

Hugh pushed his hand through his drying hair. He thought not. If Seb knew the body his little sister had been hiding he might have been less happy about sending Amy to stay with him.

'Right,' he said, making a decision. She was here to do him a favour and he was going to make damned sure he didn't do anything to embarrass her. And, judging from the way he longed to slip his hand around that slender neck and pull her closer, it was going to be quite a challenge. 'I'm going to get a shirt.'

'Where do you keep the bread?'

'Bread?'

'I want some toast,' Amy said, her brown eyes sparkling with impish amusement.

She was laughing at him again. No question. Amy knew exactly the effect she was having on him and was finding it funny. Very funny. A muscle pulsed in his jaw as he forced his mind to concentrate on what she'd asked for. 'There's a loaf in the bottom cupboard. Put a slice on for me,' he said, making for the door.

'Okay,' she said, bending over to look. 'Just the one?'

'One's fine,' he said tightly as he watched the fabric pull slightly over her round, firm buttocks. This was definitely going to be a long couple of weeks, he thought as he made a desperate retreat.

On the other hand maybe it was just the shock of the transformation that was causing the difficulty. Eventually he was going to become used to the new Amy and his libido would settle.

Wouldn't it? His fingers fumbled slightly over the buttons of his shirt. The trouble was this was *Amy* and he liked her. That put her firmly out of bounds. It was playing too close to home and it could only get messy.

By the time he returned to the kitchen Amy was seated on one of the high bar stools, a piece of toast in her hand. 'You know, Hugh, your kitchen is a complete disgrace. You've got all these fancy gadgets and nothing to eat.'

He slid on the seat opposite. 'I told you I eat out.'

'Not for breakfast,' she replied, smearing a second piece of toast with butter. And then she thought aloud, her eyes opening in disbelief, 'Surely you don't stay out every night. What's the point of having a house at all then?'

Hugh shifted uncomfortably but forced himself to smile. 'Not every night, minx. I normally try to get to the gym before work and I grab breakfast there. Is that okay with you?'

She smiled sunnily. 'That's fine. I'm only interested because I know it's the kind of thing your mum will want me to find out. She's very concerned about your domestic arrangements.'

'Now you can reassure her.'

'Perhaps,' she teased. 'Why the gym?'

Hugh reached for his mug of coffee and drank deeply. 'It de-stresses me. It's a good way to start the day with a clear mind.'

'You mean it burns off the alcohol,' she said tartly. 'Do you know you have three bottles of wine in your fridge but only a dribble of milk? No cheese. No salad.'

'Unopened bottles of wine,' he said, standing up. 'If you're looking for signs of my debauchery, you ought to check on the empties. Are you still intending to make your own way to Harpur-Laithwaite?'

Amy picked up her empty plate. 'It's probably better if you want me to look like a bona fide temp. What time does Barbara get in each morning?'

'Between seven and half past.'

She paused at the dishwasher, plate in hand. 'That's far too early!'

'That's when I start.'

'Maybe, but—'

'No buts. The whole point is that you're there when I am. If Sonya knows you don't get in until nine, then I'm a sitting duck.'

Amy opened the dishwasher door and placed her plate in the rack. 'I understand that, but I still think an agency temp wouldn't appear on the first morning that early. Barbara's around today to show me what to do, so it won't matter, will it?' She turned round and looked at him questioningly.

'I suppose not,' he said, swiftly knotting his tie. 'But after today you're going to have to make sure you're not late. That's what I'm paying you for.'

'Tomorrow you can text me when you're about to leave the gym and I'll appear like a genie.' She smiled. 'I'm beginning to think I'll have earnt these clothes.'

'Don't worry, you will do,' he said dryly, before reaching for his briefcase. 'Barbara's only going to be in until eleven so make sure you get in by nine. At the latest.'

If she'd needed any confirmation she looked different it would have come in the way the suited man leaving Harpur-Laithwaite held the door open for her. In her previous life such a thing had rarely occurred and never with the obsequious attention he displayed.

It was a confidence-building moment and she found she needed it as she followed Barbara Shelton along the plush carpeted corridors.

She hated to admit it but there was something very intimidating about Hugh's obvious success. It was one thing to sit about in Henley trading friendly insults with him, it was another to face the heir apparent on his own territory. It was a dimension to Hugh she'd never really considered.

'Hugh Balfour—handsome, wealthy, playboy type' ran easily off her lips, but he was also responsible for people. Real people. For their careers and by extension their happiness. It made him seem quite important.

'It's a terrible time for me to be away,' Barbara was saying in her precise voice. 'I wondered whether I should cancel, but then I would be letting so many other people down.'

Amy teetered after her, desperately trying to keep up and make sympathetic noises at the same time. 'I'm sure Hugh...Mr, I mean Dr Balfour wouldn't want you to do that.'

Barbara didn't seem to notice her confusion over what to call him. She continued at a breathtakingly fast pace and spoke as quickly as she walked. 'I'm so glad you're able to take over. A friend of the family is such a sensible idea...in the circumstances. As far as one can foresee these

things, there shouldn't be any major crises while I'm away.
I've also put together a file on everything you'll need to
know.'

'Right.'

'There's the usual Thursday meeting, of course.' She
turned another corner. 'I've left notes on that. And anything else ask Fiona. She's Adrian Dunn's PA and a very
good girl. Through that door and at the end of the corridor.
I'll introduce you later. She's on extension two two seven.'

'Two two seven,' Amy repeated dutifully with very little
expectation of remembering, as her mind was completely
taken up by the confusion of corridors. With every twist
and turn she felt more and more overwhelmed. And more
scared. Hugh was relying on her not to let him down and
she wasn't at all sure she was up to the job.

'It's in the folder.'

Amy pulled her eyes away from a modern interpretation
of the River Thames at night and looked back at Barbara.
'Ah, good.'

'He likes the *Financial Times* and all the broadsheets
on his desk first thing. I always pick them up on the way
in. Try and give him the first hour or so to catch up on
what's been happening in the States overnight before putting through any calls. And this,' she said, pushing open
the door to her left, 'will be your home for the next two
weeks.'

Amy stood looking round the most spacious office she'd
ever been in. Apart from the state-of-the-art computer sitting on a pale desk, there was also a cluster of chairs
around a low coffee-table, a row of filing cabinets and a
wall of ceiling-to-floor shelves full of box files.
Meticulously tidy and excruciatingly intimidating.

She let her handbag fall onto one of the nearby chairs.
If she'd needed anything more to confirm how way out of

her depth she was, this was it. Her previous experiences as a temporary secretary had been spent tucked behind filing cabinets in rooms more accurately described as cupboards or, conversely, in wide open reception areas where draughts and people wandered at will. Nothing like this.

'If you'd like to go through and let Hugh know you're here,' Barbara said, indicating the closed door beside the filing cabinets. 'He's been waiting impatiently for you to arrive. I'll go and make some coffee before we settle down to work. How do you take yours?'

'White, one sugar.'

And then she disappeared, leaving Amy with the tricky problem of whether she should knock on the door to Hugh's office—or not. It was all a question of getting the right balance, she thought as her hand hesitated. Mockingly deferential but not rude was what she needed to aim for. *Why had she ever agreed to work for Hugh?*

In the end she went for a cursory tap before walking straight in.

And then she froze.

Her bright 'hello' dried up as she took in the sight of Sonya Laithwaite leant across the double desk, her ample chest oozing out of the top of a fuchsia-pink jacket. Amy felt the colour drain from her face and her palms became clammy.

'Here comes the cavalry,' Sonya said on a choky laugh, making no attempt to cover herself up. She twisted round on the desk. 'I know you, don't I? I'm sure I've seen you before.'

A wave of nausea washed through her. It was what Hugh and Seb had told her to expect but she hadn't really believed it. Why would any woman behave like this—particularly one who had so much to lose? For a moment Amy hesitated, slightly uncertain of what she'd actually stumbled into. Then she saw the mute appeal for help in Hugh's eyes and the feeling of sickness receded. She shut the door with an outward calm and walked further into the office.

Amazingly Sonya didn't move. She remained perched on the edge of his desk, more of her breasts outside the jacket than in. Her impeccably made-up face showed no sign of embarrassment.

'My father and your husband are friends, *Mrs* Laithwaite,' she said pointedly, waiting for some trace of discomfort to appear on the other woman's face.

There was nothing.

'Really?'

Hugh got up from his chair and walked around the table. 'This is Amelia Mitchell,' he said, putting an arm around her and pulling her up close against him. It didn't seem the natural movement of a boss towards his temporary secretary, but Amy held still. For the first time in her life she really believed Hugh needed help. It was a novel experience and she'd no intention of letting him down.

'Mitchell?' Sonya mused. 'I remember. You're Phillip's daughter.' Her coldly assessing glance passed over her new clothes. 'You've changed. You were a frumpy little thing when I last saw you.'

'You're exactly as I remember you,' Amy shot back, irritated.

Sonya's hard eyes flashed. 'Have I missed something? Good God, are you *dating* Hugh?' she asked.

'No—'

Hugh cut her off. 'A little more than that. Amy's just moved in.'

It was only the pressure of his fingers at her waist that stopped her exclaiming.

Sonya flicked herself off the edge of the table and stood

looking down at Amy as though she were something a cat might have dragged in. 'Does Calantha know?'

'Of course,' Hugh answered.

Slowly Sonya began to button up her jacket. 'Fascinating.' Her eyes were glittering and suspicious. 'And I thought you were bringing Calantha to Richard's party.'

'I'm bringing Amy.'

Amy stiffened slightly. What game was Hugh playing now? It was one thing to agree to work as his secretary, but this was something else. She was now being cast as live-in lover and decorative airhead. *What had happened to Calantha?*

'I see,' Sonya said, walking calmly over to the door.

Amy stood immobile as she passed them. At the door Sonya paused. 'She'll never cope with you, Hugh. There'll always be someone, sweetheart,' she said patronisingly, turning her eyes on Amy. 'A new excitement. A new adventure. We're two of a kind, Hugh and I. If you take my advice you won't unpack too much.'

She shut the door behind her with a quiet click.

There was silence until Amy was quite sure she'd heard a second click indicating the door to the adjoining office had just closed. She pulled away.

'What are you playing at?' she snapped. 'This isn't quite the line of secretarial duties I imagined. What's happened to Calantha?'

'Quiet,' he instructed. 'She might be listening.'

'No.' Amy flung open the door to reveal the empty outer office. 'All safe. What's going on? What are you doing?'

'I'm glad you got here when you did,' he remarked, walking round the desk and sitting back in his chair. 'I was about to get an eyeful.'

'How can you joke about it? It isn't funny. Think of

how Richard would be feeling if he'd walked in instead of me?'

'I am. That's what this is all about,' he returned. 'Where's Barbara?'

'Gone to get us all a coffee.'

'Bloody bad timing.'

'She wasn't to know that. Stop prevaricating. What's happened between you and Calantha since you left me this morning?'

Hugh leant forward and clicked on his email. 'Come and look.' He leant back in his chair. 'There's no fury like a woman scorned,' he said softly.

'What did you *do* last night?' she asked, moving round the table.

'Nothing. I rather think that's the problem.'

Her eyes scanned his message. 'It doesn't read like that. Who's the other woman you're showing too much interest in?'

'You.'

Amy's heart thumped erratically 'You can't be serious.'

'Read it for yourself.' He shrugged. 'Apparently I'm paying too much attention to you and not considering her needs. She's concerned about my unwillingness to commit and thinks we should take a break.'

'I can read.'

He leant forward and closed the message. 'She's right about that. I'm completely unprepared to commit but I needed her for the party. Still, at least you're here.' He looked at her speculatively.

Amy looked up, horror-struck. 'Don't look at me. I'm not going with you. That's completely outside my remit.'

'We don't have much choice,' he said smugly. 'I've already told Sonya I'm bringing you.'

'Find someone else.'

'Like how? I've been dating Callie since last October. I can't suddenly produce someone else and pretend I'm in love with her instead. Sonya will never believe it's serious.'

'Then you'd better try and change Calantha's mind,' Amy suggested, moving away.

'Only an engagement ring's going to change her mind. But you are the perfect wild card. We go back years.'

He was serious! His impossibly handsome face showed absolutely no sign of teasing. She stared at him for a full minute before she managed, 'You can't honestly expect me to agree.'

'Why not?'

Amy shook her head, amazed he'd even asked the question. 'Why can't you take any of the women you've dated before? Ring someone up. What about the blonde one you went out with before Calantha? Imogen, was that her name?'

Hugh picked up a pencil and tapped it on the table. 'Sonya wouldn't need to be a member of Mensa to know I wasn't serious. Besides, what excuse would I give Imogen for behaving as though she were the love of my life after I've not contacted her for months?'

'You could try the truth.'

'You're mad. Of course I couldn't. You met Imogen. She's not the kind of woman built for discretion.'

'That's your problem,' Amy said, heading for the door.

'No, it's Richard's.'

Amy paused, her hand on the doorknob. The only reason she was here at all was because of Richard. And she couldn't even comfort herself now by telling herself Hugh was exaggerating his problem with Sonya.

But to pretend she was Hugh's girlfriend?

At fifteen she'd have jumped at the chance, but since

then experience had taught her a little wisdom. To be the focus of Hugh's attention, to have him pretend to adore her, was going to lay her open to believing it. He would walk away from the charade completely unscathed—but she might not.

And who would believe it? Her brown eyes clouded with worry. She didn't want people looking at her and wondering what Hugh saw in her. There was her pride involved in this too. Hugh was a racehorse kind of a man and, after her recent experience with Greg, she felt more like a pit pony. 'No one will believe you're involved with me.'

'Sonya did. She was angry.' Hugh twisted his pencil between long fingers, watching her. 'You walking in when you did was inspired. You're the perfect candidate. You're Phillip's daughter and Seb's sister. I've known you for years. You're living in my house. I've never had a woman actually move in before. It's perfect.'

It was rather like being in quicksand. She felt as if she were slowly being sucked under—and there was very little she could do about it. 'But I'm not blonde. You always go for blondes.'

Hugh looked up, startled. 'I what?'

'Chrisse, Paulette, Rowena, then it was Stefi, I think. After that it was Imogen and then Calantha. All blonde. All at least five feet seven. Don't you think you'd be straining incredulity a bit far to suddenly pitch up with me?'

Hugh's eyes crinkled and Amy's stomach did its habitual flip. 'I'd no idea you were keeping a record.'

'I'm not your type,' she said a little desperately.

'But you might be the sort of person I'd choose when I'm serious. That's what we'll make everyone believe. It's perfect.'

'It isn't. It's—'

'Shh,' Hugh said suddenly, turning his face towards the door. 'I think this is Barbara. We can discuss this later.'

He stood up and opened the door.

Barbara looked ruffled. 'I've just seen Mrs Laithwaite in the corridor. Is—?'

'Amy successfully routed the enemy,' Hugh interjected.

'Well done,' Barbara said, visibly relaxing. She turned and busied herself with the coffee, before picking up Hugh's and bringing it through to his office. 'I'm so sorry I wasn't here. I'd no idea Mrs Laithwaite was in the building this morning. No idea at all.'

'Amy did excellently. In fact, it couldn't have been better.'

Barbara put his coffee down on the walnut coaster. 'Well, that's a relief. Right, if you'd like to come with me, Amy, I'll take you through my notes and show you where everything is kept.'

Amy threw a glance at Hugh that she hoped told him the matter was far from settled. *Hugh was outrageous.* The more she thought about it, the more impossible it all was. He couldn't seriously expect her to pose as his girlfriend in front of her godfather and countless others who knew her father well. Aside from the fact no one with a brain cell would believe he'd have traded Calantha for her, she wasn't at all keen to set herself up for the humiliating aftermath of being known as one of Hugh's exes—even if her heart did emerge unscathed.

Amy moved her red handbag and sat down in the cream armchair. She couldn't do it. He was going to have to think of something else.

'Now,' Barbara said, bringing across an alarming pile of box files, 'we don't have long, so let's begin with the file I've put together for you. Keep it near you like a bible. It should answer all your questions.'

An hour and a half later, with her coffee cold beside her, Amy had to concede Barbara's notes were meticulous. She even had a small card box with the names of people Hugh dealt with regularly, together with notes on their significant others and dining preferences. Everything to keep Hugh's world revolving smoothly.

Amy smiled to herself as she flicked through her 'bible'. Until Sonya had burst onto the scene everything had been made so easy for Hugh. He probably didn't even realise how much his secretary did for him. Just one more adoring woman in his fan club.

'So, will you manage?' Barbara asked with a quick glance at her wrist-watch.

'I should think so. I can cope with Word easily enough and you've left me notes on everything else.'

'And Hugh will have to help you if you get stuck,' she said, reaching for her large beige handbag. 'Fiona will too, of course, but she'll be a little nervous now.'

'Why?'

Barbara hesitated. 'In view of you agreeing to pose as Hugh's girlfriend at the weekend, I thought it prudent to mention it to some of the senior support staff.'

Agreed! She'd done no such thing.

'I told them you're living together now and that you've agreed to help out in the office while I'm away.' She looked a little concerned at the expression on Amy's face. 'It may make you a little more isolated because they'll naturally be nervous in case you pass anything back. He's the boss, after all.'

'No one's going to believe I'm his girlfriend. Not in place of Calantha.'

'I don't see why,' Barbara said unanswerably, rummaging through her handbag. 'It's only for a couple of weeks, after all. While you're here. From what he tells me it does seem like the perfect solution.'

But that was from his perspective, Amy thought, irritated. Posing as Hugh's girlfriend was a step too far. *This was so unfair.* It made her want to scream and thump something. He'd deliberately told Barbara in order to manipulate her into going along with it.

'Now, this is the telephone number of my mother. I'll be there if you need me.'

Amy reached out and took the paper. 'I thought you were on holiday?'

'Not exactly. My sister and her family are coming over from Canada for the first time in eight years. We are having a huge family gathering. If it was anything else I'd have postponed it until after Richard Laithwaite's retirement party.'

'Oh.'

Barbara looked around the office. 'Well, that's it. Time I was leaving. I've got a flight up to Scotland this afternoon.' Amy nodded. 'Do telephone if there's anything at all you need help with.'

'I will.'

Still she hesitated. 'If you need to contact anyone connected with Hugh's private life, you'll find them in a notebook in the bottom left-hand drawer of my desk.'

'Like this one?' Amy asked holding up her 'bible'.

'Not quite,' she said, with an unexpectedly mischievous smile. 'It's an original little black book.'

That had to be worth seeing. As soon as Barbara had left the room Amy walked over to the computer and stretched down to open the drawer. Nestling under some papers was a small leatherbound book. She flicked the pages. There was more information here than even she'd been able to glean over the years.

'S—Stevenson, Paulette. Birthday 24th May. Likes sushi.' Not too much to go on there. Other entries had far more information, but then Paulette's reign as Hugh appendage had been brief.

It was wicked but she couldn't resist a quick peep at 'R—Rainford-Smythe, Calantha. Birthday 29th October. Designer. Prefers platinum to gold. Doesn't eat red meat. Likes yellow flowers (adds energy to a room).' It was tempting to add 'Left you in the lurch. Wants an engagement ring.' After the smallest deliberation she decided not to.

CHAPTER FIVE

By THE time Hugh stuck his head round the door just over an hour later Amy was feeling quite confident in her new role. She'd effortlessly fielded a telephone call from an irate Mr Fletcher, who'd wanted to be rung back first thing after the weekend break, and had nearly finished the confidential report Barbara had left her to type. She'd also acquired a new respect for Hugh. Something other than an appreciation of the sinful glint in his blue eyes.

She'd always known he was clever. He'd been a 'straight A' student without much effort on his part, had left Oxford with a first in Philosophy of Mathematics and followed it with a PhD. All high-powered stuff. But she'd never given much thought to how successful he was now. On his advice people risked millions.

'Have you nearly finished?'

'Nearly. I've just got the conclusion to type.' Amy looked up, her fingers poised over the keyboard.

'Let's go and get some lunch.'

'Don't know if I have the time. I work for this really demanding man who keeps me chained to my PC,' she quipped, forgetting for a moment she was angry.

'Stand up to him,' Hugh suggested, moving around the edge of her desk and shutting her file.

'You don't know how much I'd love to.' Amy flicked on the 'save' button and closed down the document. 'He's a real toad.' She looked up at him, her eyes narrowed accusingly. 'Did you tell Barbara to start spreading rumours about us?'

'Yes.'

His baldly stated admission rather took the wind out of her sails. It was disarming. It made it difficult to keep up the momentum of righteous indignation, but she gave it her best effort. 'So I wouldn't be able to refuse?'

'Something like that,' he admitted, the grooves on his cheeks deepening as he obviously fought back a smile.

'That's not fair.'

'No. But I'm a desperate man.' He reached down to pull her out of her typing chair. 'Come and have some lunch. I can argue away all your objections then. If I put my mind to it I can be very persuasive.'

Taking time to pick up her handbag, Amy let him steer her out of the office, aware of the way the door at the end of the corridor opened a fraction. She could almost imagine the curious eyes squinting through the crack to get a glimpse of them together.

It was so unfair. He'd made it so difficult for her to refuse without feeling guilty.

Hugh always did this to her. He always managed to make you feel you were the one being unreasonable if you didn't fall in with his plans. But not this time. This time she really had to resist him.

She surreptitiously looked across at the way his dark hair nestled against the top of his crisp white shirt collar and imagined the muscle tone he was hiding beneath his formal charcoal jacket. What was the *matter* with her? She knew far too much about him to fall for the Hugh charm— *surely*?

Hugh was a walking disaster. He never stuck with anyone. He was like a boy in a sweetie shop. So many sweets, so much to choose from.

And you couldn't blame him. Women seemed to lie down in front of him begging to be walked over. But not her. Never her. She wanted a man who would stick with her. Someone who just might possibly be around to help parent his children until they left home.

She wasn't immune to his innate charm, to his kindness and the pure, unadulterated sex appeal of the man—but she knew he wasn't what she wanted. What she needed. And for her own survival she couldn't allow herself to be seduced into forgetting it. Not for a moment. She knew he could really hurt her. And quite frankly she'd been hurt enough.

'Where are we going?'

'It depends what you'd like. Do you fancy Italian? Chinese? Or we could stop by at Ichiro's,' he suggested, holding open the door for her. 'It's a new sushi bar that's just opened up.'

Amy looked up at him critically. 'You know, you must waste a fortune on lunches,' she scolded. 'Normal people would grab a roll and sit in the sunshine.'

'We can do that too.' He smiled, placing his hand in the small of her back and guiding her through the impressive reception area. He paused momentarily to say, 'Good afternoon, Sangita,' to the woman who was manning the desk. Amy was keenly aware of her double take and the whispered aside she made to her younger colleague.

'We'll go wherever you like. I'm trying to charm you into getting my own way, remember?'

At least he admitted it. But then that was part of his technique. He'd lull you into a false sense of security and then hit you hard in the solar plexus. How else had she ended up typing his PhD all those years ago? Nothing much had changed.

The bright July sunshine stung her eyes as it bounced off the pavement and the smell of car fumes hung heavy in the air.

'Let's get off the main street. There's a nice place round here.'

He led her through a maze of backstreets and ended up in a small courtyard with tables spilling out across the newly cobbled surface. 'How did you know this was here?' she asked, amazed at the unexpectedness of it.

'This is an area that's being targeted for regeneration. I just looked at the plans and came for an explore one day. They do the best egg-mayonnaise baguette I've ever tasted.'

'Great,' she said, settling herself at one of the metal tables. 'And can I have a large glass of cold water?' She looked up and grinned. 'I assume, since you're trying to be charming, you're paying? I only mention it because I haven't any money.'

He disappeared inside leaving Amy to wonder how she was going to get out of posing as his girlfriend. In a way it didn't matter so much around the office if people thought they were involved, but it did matter where her real life and his overlapped. What would her godfather think? His mother? If his mother got to hear of it she'd be ordering the wedding cake before he could turn round twice.

She moved her chair so she sat more directly in the shade of the blue sun umbrella and squinted up at the wispy clouds. His mother was probably going to be her best line of defence.

'They've put lemon in your water. Is that okay?' he asked as he returned.

'Fine.' She took a sip. 'Oh, that's so cold. Lovely.'

'They'll bring the baguettes out in a minute. Now,' Hugh said, sitting down opposite her, 'you can shout at me if you think it will help.'

Amy looked at the effortless charm that was Hugh. He really had this whole thing taped. He'd just the right amount of glint in those deep blue eyes, just the right relaxation in his lithe body and just the right level of confidence in his own ability to convince.

'I can't do it, Hugh,' she said simply. 'We know too many of the same people. The news that we're an item would follow us for ever. It would be horrible.'

She took a sip of her cold water and waited for him to say something. He said nothing and she risked a glance across. His fingers were curved loosely round his tall glass and he was watching her curiously. Just waiting.

'Can you just imagine what your mother would say?' She let her finger slide up the glass, brushing away the droplets of condensation.

'I think she'd say it was the first sign of good taste I've ever shown.'

Amy looked across at him, expecting to see laughter in his eyes. That there wasn't any confused her a little. 'What about Seb?'

His mouth quirked a little at that but he answered calmly. 'It's just a party. Why—?' He broke off as a young girl appeared carrying two plates.

'Two baguettes. Sorry to have kept you waiting.'

Amy moved her elbow so the waitress could put her plate beside her. 'Thank you.'

'And one for you,' she said to Hugh, her eyes openly admiring. Suddenly Amy wanted to laugh. If he could bottle whatever it was he had, he'd earn a fortune. It was quite ridiculous how he drew women to him like a magnet.

She watched the girl leave and then looked back at Hugh. 'You think I'm being really silly, don't you?'

The sides of his mouth curved. 'It's a very salutary experience to have a woman not want to go out with me.'

'And probably way overdue,' she quipped back, unable to stop herself.

His face became serious. 'I know you, Amy. You won't back out now. You've seen Sonya and just how far she's prepared to go. You may not think my neck's worth saving, but you'll do it for Richard.'

Amy twisted her plate round so the cucumber was on the far side. He was right.

'It would destroy him if he thought his wife was cheating on him with me,' Hugh said quietly.

Knowing how Richard had become almost a surrogate father to Hugh, she didn't doubt it. It would be a double betrayal. In her head she could see her mother slumped over the kitchen table when she'd first heard her father was leaving them. She could still hear the racking sobs and feel the inadequacy as she'd realised she was powerless to help. She couldn't sit by and do nothing to help her godfather.

'What's the worst that could happen?' Hugh asked quietly, his eyes on her face.

It was a question she didn't like to think about, let alone answer. She didn't really know what was frightening her the most—that she might start falling for Hugh in a way she couldn't control or that people would talk about her.

Amy bit into her baguette and bought herself a little more time before answering. 'I suppose,' she said slowly, 'I suppose I don't want everyone thinking I'm your bimbo. It's humiliating.'

Her answer surprised him. She could tell from the way his eyes narrowed and then crinkled at the edges. 'Impossible. You're not a blonde.'

'You know what I mean. I don't want people talking about me and speculating what you see in me. Why don't you use your little black book and find someone more suitable?'

'I don't have one.'

'You do,' Amy returned, her fingers playing with the water glass. 'Barbara's the perfect secretary. She's kept your life fully documented and all your contacts noted.' His forehead furrowed in confusion and she took pity on him. 'I'll show you when we get back to the office. I just think you could do better than me. That's all.'

Hugh sat back in his chair and watched her. Amy was like no other woman he knew. She could be so many different things all within a second. At one moment she was warm and funny, the next she was prickly and defensive.

And she was difficult to read. But not this time. This time he was in no doubt what she was feeling. Her petite frame was held stiffly and her hand movements were jerky and uncomfortable. Considering they were such friends, had known each other for such a long time, it was strange she was so reluctant to partner him to Richard's retirement party.

It was also strange how much he wanted her to. Something had shifted in the last twenty-four hours he could never have foreseen. Amy had somehow ceased to be Seb's little sister and had metamorphosed into someone in her own right.

She was beautiful. Her hair hung in a shiny dark bob and her brown eyes held a mystery he hadn't dreamt was there. In one way she was so familiar and yet in another she was someone he didn't know at all but realised he'd like to. She also had the lowest self-esteem of anyone he'd met—and that really fascinated him.

Why would someone as sparky and beautiful as Amy Mitchell feel so badly about herself?

'Amy,' he began carefully, watching her face for any signs that might give a window into what she was feeling, 'there isn't anyone better than you. I trust you. We're friends. And I need your help.'

He watched the conflicting emotions travel over her intense face.

'If I go to the retirement party...'

'Yes?' he prompted.

'Would that be it? Just the one evening?'

He felt the guilt spread through his body. He'd already involved her more than that when he'd encouraged Barbara to tell Fiona he was living with Amy. He'd known the information would disseminate from there and that, long before the weekend, news of his break-up with Calantha would be common knowledge.

When he'd drawn Sangita's attention to them leaving he'd done so because he'd wanted her to see them together. Already Amy would be thought of as his new girlfriend.

'I need you until I can sort out this business with Sonya.'

'But how long will that be?'

The desperation in her voice twisted the knife again. He'd never seen Amy so uncomfortable. 'After the party she and Richard are going on holiday. When they come back she'll have no reason to come into Harpur-Laithwaite's and I will make it abundantly clear to her I want nothing to do with her. If I have to I'll threaten her with an injunction.'

'Will that work?'

'I hope so. With a bit of luck it won't get that far. Sonya can't want Richard to divorce her. She's very expensive tastes.'

Amy sat back in her chair, the umbrella casting a shadow across her face. 'Can I think about it?'

'Not really, Amy,' he said, the guilt ripping into him now. 'By the time we get back to the office I doubt there'll be anyone left who won't know we're an item.'

He couldn't see her expression as clearly now but he

saw her fingers clench together in her lap. 'You haven't left me with much choice, then, have you?'

'No. I'm sorry.'

'Good old Amy to the rescue. It's nice to know I have my uses.'

Her voice dripped a weary sarcasm. Hugh moved his chair so he could see her clearly. 'Why do you say it like that?'

She gave a half-shrug. 'It's nothing.'

'Yes, it is. Why do you talk about yourself like that?' Her eyes flew up to his, half startled. 'Who was it messed you up, Amy?'

'W-Why…?'

'Someone's hurt you. I must have missed that. Was it that man at Christmas…?'

She shook her head, the dark hair swinging. 'Greg. Not really. At least not any more.'

This felt important. He watched her. Saw the way her fingers twisted in her lap, the nervous biting of her lip. 'Tell me.'

Amy looked up. 'About Greg?'

He nodded.

The hands in her lap twisted again. 'There's nothing much to tell. No big story. He found someone else he liked better than me. That's all.'

'Someone you knew?' he prompted.

'No.' Her brown eyes flashed at him. 'Just someone more interesting, more exciting. The usual thing men move on for. What's this got to do with anything anyway? The fact that Greg cheated on me and then dumped me has got nothing to do with not wanting to play-act your girlfriend. Or—'

She broke off and took a sip of water.

Hugh didn't dare interrupt her. He sat patiently and waited.

'I suppose it does—in a way,' she said at last. 'I didn't like the sympathy. Or being talked over. I didn't like the way people looked at me and gossiped about me.'

'And that's how you see yourself? As someone who was dumped?' he asked baldly.

'N-no. Of course not.'

'But you don't like being talked about?'

Amy broke a bit off her baguette and ate it. More, Hugh suspected, as a way of avoiding having to answer his question. He pushed his own empty plate away from him and thought. 'So, are you concerned about what people will say when we let it be known we're no longer together?'

Her brown eyes looked at him and then skitted away again. But he'd seen enough. 'That's easily solved. You can dump me.' He drained the last of his glass. 'We'll let it be known I'm just as obnoxious as you always thought I was. I will even undertake to look suitably broken-hearted for at least a week afterwards. Will that help?'

Amy gave a half-laugh.

He reached out his hand. 'Do we have a deal?'

'Three weeks heartbroken,' she challenged. 'Minimum.'

'Two.'

'Two,' Amy conceded, placing her hand in his. 'And you get to tell your mother.'

He gave a crack of laughter. 'Agreed. Have you finished all you want of your baguette?'

'Yes.'

'Then let's go back to work.' He waited until she was standing beside him and reached out to touch her arm. 'You know, I won't let any of this hurt you.'

Her tender eyes brimmed up with tears and it shook him

to see it. 'I know you'll do your best. I still wish you could think of someone else.'

'From my "little black book"?'

The tears vanished in a gurgle of laughter. 'Absolutely. Come on, let's go back to work.'

He nodded and they headed back to Harpur-Laithwaite. Amy glanced up at him and smiled to herself. Somehow she'd agreed to do exactly what he wanted. That should have irritated her but it didn't. After Sonya's performance this morning she couldn't doubt he needed her. Besides, it would be worth something for their friends to believe she'd finished with him. It appealed to her sense of humour.

As they entered the reception area Hugh laid a warning hand on her arm. 'Richard,' Hugh said quietly.

'Where?'

'Over by the desk.'

Amy spun round at the same moment Richard Laithwaite looked up and saw them. His face lit into a broad smile.

'I've just been up to your office, Hugh,' he began with a glance in the direction of his friend. 'I wanted to see Amy. Find out how you managed on your first morning. How are you, my dear?'

'Fine,' she answered as he kissed her on the cheek.

'You're looking well.'

'I am.' Actually so did he. If she hadn't known about his angina she wouldn't have guessed it.

Richard took her by the arm and led her towards the stairs. 'Let's go and have a coffee in Hugh's office. I haven't seen you since Easter. And that was only a flying visit because Sonya wasn't well enough to come with me. Do you remember?'

All the way across the wide marble reception area Amy was acutely aware of people watching her. She felt very uncomfortable. She'd never felt that way with her godfather before. All she could think of was Sonya's ample bosoms pouring out of her fuchsia jacket that morning.

'I saw Seb for lunch last month,' he continued, blithely unaware of her turmoil. 'That production company of his appears to be taking off. He's had some very good reviews for that last documentary.'

Amy looked back at Hugh, glad to see he was following close behind. 'I think so. He's doing something on stately homes right now.'

'And Luke?'

'Is busy. His two years in Africa will be up at the end of the year. As far as I know he still plans on coming home.'

Richard nodded. 'That's good. There's a crying shortage of good paediatricians. I don't know why he took off like that.'

'I'll get the coffee,' Hugh said behind them.

Richard's eyes glinted. 'Make sure you get a few of those double-chocolate-chip cookies Barbara buys especially for you.' He turned back to Amy. 'No one else is allowed them. I'm sure she thinks we don't know they're kept in the top right-hand cupboard.'

Hugh smiled. 'I'll tell her you've found them.'

'Don't get anything like that from my PA. She thinks I should watch my cholesterol.' Richard guided Amy along the corridor and into Hugh's office. 'Now you sit there and tell me how you're liking London.'

'I haven't seen much of it yet,' Amy replied, desperately hoping Hugh wouldn't be long with the coffee. How did Hugh manage this, day after day? She was terrified she'd suddenly spurt out something about Sonya.

'Hugh tells me you're looking for a flat.'

'I hope so. I'll save as much as possible from what I earn here to put down as my deposit.'

'Don't worry about that,' he said, holding up a hand. 'I'll see you right for that. I didn't realise your father hadn't thought of it. I suppose he's got other things on his mind.'

'Yes.'

Richard's astute eyes took in more than she wanted. 'Lynda isn't the kind to share. I should have thought of that.'

It was strange how he could be so observant about some things and so obtuse about his own marriage. Perhaps it was because he needed Sonya? Maybe he really loved her? Amy bit her lip. If so, that was sad. He was going to be hurt.

'It's time you let go of your mother's house. There are far too many memories bound up in that old place and not all of them are good.'

Hugh opened the door. 'Someone had just boiled the kettle so it didn't take long.'

'I was just saying,' Richard remarked, passing Amy a fine bone china mug, 'that it's time Amy sold that cottage.' He reached for a biscuit. 'Moved away from Henley. There's very few of the old crowd left, I imagine.'

'Hugh's mum's still there.'

'Ah, yes, Moira,' he agreed, a wistful edge to his voice. 'I don't think she'll ever move. Do you, Hugh?'

He shook his head. 'Unlikely.'

'After your father died I tried to persuade her to move to London but she wasn't having any of it.' Richard pulled himself back to the present. 'I do wish I'd remembered you were starting today. I could have brought Sonya over to say hello. She was in first thing. She's got bits and pieces to do in town before the party.'

He smiled and Amy felt her stomach lurch. She didn't dare look across at Hugh.

'Perhaps we could get together for dinner one night? All four of us.'

Hugh put his mug down on the coffee-table. 'Will you have time before the party?'

'Perhaps not,' Richard agreed regretfully. 'But after Sonya and I are back from Florida—'

'That would be lovely,' Amy cut in quickly. It wouldn't matter by then. Hugh would have dealt with Sonya and she'd have moved on to find her own flat. Hopefully.

Richard glanced down at his wrist-watch. 'Will you be at the party?'

'Y-yes, Hugh—'

'Will drive you over. Excellent. I told him to mention it to you.'

It was cowardly but Amy couldn't face telling her god-father she was going as Hugh's girlfriend. Apparently Hugh wasn't in any rush to tell him either because he said nothing.

Richard didn't notice. 'Sonya's putting so much work into the arrangements. She's talked of nothing else for weeks.' He put his own mug down on the table. 'Sonya finds it difficult being on her own so much. It'll be better for her when I've finally retired.'

He smiled and Amy felt an urge to cry. Richard had no idea his wife was perfectly happy to find amusement else-where.

'We'll be able to do some of the travelling she's so keen on,' he said, standing up. 'Right, back to the grindstone. I'm not finished until Friday.'

As the door shut behind him Amy whispered, 'That was awful.'

Hugh stood up abruptly. 'That's why we're doing this.'

'I know. But why can't he see what Sonya's like?'

'She's very careful how she behaves around him. You'd think she idolised him. It's horrid. I agree,' he said, looking at her face. He leant down and carelessly stroked her cheek. 'But we're doing all we can. Even so, I think it's inevitable he's going to be hurt.'

Amy watched Hugh disappear into his own office. He was right. It *was* inevitable Richard would be hurt. For the first time since she'd arrived at Harpur-Laithwaite she was genuinely glad she was there.

'Ms Mitchell?' a young man asked as he opened the door to the outer office midway through the afternoon.

'Yes?' Amy looked up from behind her computer screen.

'I'm sorry we missed a couple of Dr Balfour's letters in the mail room this morning. They got muddled up with someone else's post and have only just come back down. One of them's marked "private" so we was a bit worried it might be important, like.'

'Don't worry about it. I'll take them through in a moment,' she said, reaching out her hand. 'Thank you.'

The man backed himself out of the room as though he were leaving royalty. If she could have been sure it was simply by virtue of her status as Hugh Balfour's temporary PA she'd have enjoyed it. Instead her mouth twisted in distaste. The news she was sleeping with the boss had obviously spread exactly as Hugh'd predicted. She felt trapped into a situation she wasn't comfortable with. No doubt he'd return to the mail room with some comment like, 'She's very short,' or, 'Not as pretty as the other one.'

She slipped open the top of the letters with a long ruler and gave the contents a cursory glance. They were unimportant mailshots, which she promptly consigned to the waste-paper bin. But the parcel was handwritten, firmly taped and squishy. She pressed it with her fingers. It was marked 'Private. Addressee only'. Her stomach twisted over in anticipation. If it turned out not to be from Sonya she was going to feel let down. She reached for her scissors and cut the top of the packet off.

Lifting the packet up by the corners, she gave it a shake and watched, fascinated, as a flash of purple fell on the table. Her first thought was, *More knickers*, but then she noticed the underwiring.

A bra! Almost. It wasn't designed for support. It was designed with the sole purpose of being removed. *Good grief.* She pursed her lips and held the bra up by one of the narrow straps, wondering what Hugh did with Sonya's gifts. She waited until the light clicked off on the telephone and she knew he wasn't speaking to anyone. Tapping lightly, she opened the door and held the bra between thumb and forefinger.

'This was mislaid in the mail room. I suppose it matches the panties.'

Hugh looked up from his sheet of figures. He closed his eyes briefly and then looked back at Amy. 'That explains what Sonya was going on about this morning. She kept asking if I'd liked her present.'

'What did you do with the panties?'

'Filing cabinet under "K" for knickers,' he replied, sitting back in his chair, linking his fingers behind his head and stretching out his spine.

'Where do you want this, then? Under "B" for bra?'

'Unless you've got any better suggestions.'

Amy went across and opened the filing cabinet. Under 'K' she found the purple mesh panties and pulled them out. 'These aren't knickers. It's a thong,' she called back. 'They ought to be under "T".'

'I don't really care.'

She walked back and stood in his office doorway. 'You can't keep these in here. Suppose someone finds them?'

'Where else do you suggest?'

'Can't you throw them away?'

He grinned. 'I'd love to see the cleaner's face if I put them in the waste-basket.'

'I didn't mean that. Take them home and get rid of them.'

'I'm not taking them home,' he said firmly, the lines on his face hard and uncompromising.

She couldn't really blame him for that. 'All right, then, you'd better let me have them. I'll keep them in the bottom drawer of Barbara's desk and she can think of what to do with them,' Amy said briskly, bundling them together. 'Then if anyone finds them they'll assume they must be mine. Well, almost. If I were thinking of a breast enlargement,' she said, holding up the transparent bra.

Hugh laughed obediently, but it was forced. Inside his head alarming images were springing into life as he wondered what Amy would look like in sexy underwear. Not that she needed to bother with it anyway. She had firm breasts with tight, budding nipples. In the black T-shirt she was wearing today she'd obviously decided to wear something. The effect was different, but the shadow of a cleavage was just as sexy.

What was happening to him? He forced his eyes to look away, but the image of Amy clad in something very similar to the garments she was waving about in the air just refused to go away. He'd known her for years, spent hours in her company, but never been affected by her. Not like this.

Sonya undressing in his office just didn't figure anywhere in his fantasies, but if you replaced the woman with

Amy—it had distinct possibilities. In fact more than possibilities. It could very easily become a fixation with him unless he stopped this now.

He was under pressure. That was all it was. Once this retirement party was over everything would return to normal and all his normal desires would slip back into their customary place.

Amy balled the underwear in her hand. 'I can't see why she's bothering to do this. Surely she must find it embarrassing.'

He kept his eyes firmly back on the figures on the sheet in front of him. 'She doesn't find anything embarrassing.' It sounded more offhand than he'd intended but he didn't dare look up. Not again. He didn't want to feel any of the things he'd been feeling for the last few moments.

Hugh heard Amy shut the filing-cabinet drawer. He allowed his eyes to flick up briefly and caught sight of that perfect bottom. *How could he have missed it?* There was nothing overt, nothing outrageous in what she'd chosen to wear. Not like Sonya. Not even like Calantha. Callie dressed to be looked at, but with Amy you didn't so much notice the clothes as her. She was unexpectedly beautiful. Surprisingly so.

And she was vulnerable. To even begin to think of acting on these new impulses would break every code he'd put in place for himself. Amy was born for the 'for better, for worse', for ever kind of relationship and he knew he wasn't capable of that kind of commitment. Didn't want it.

'Hugh?' Amy turned round suddenly.

He felt foolish. Caught looking like a schoolboy. 'Yes?'

'Is it just you she does this with?' She held up her fist, clutching the underwear.

'What do you mean?'

Amy shook her head. 'I don't know really. I just wondered whether she did this because...well, because she thinks you like this sort of thing. Or whether she does it because she does. And if it's because she does, then it's quite possible you're not the only one. Do you see what I mean?'

'Does it make much difference?'

'It might to Richard.'

It was all she said. Then she shut the door. He tapped his pencil on the table and let her words revolve round his head. It was an aspect of the problem he'd not considered before. It was a possibility. What he couldn't decide was whether it changed anything.

He tried to concentrate on the figures before him. They didn't seem to make much sense and he put down the pencil with irritation. He stood up and walked over to the window. He had to keep focused. What was important was Richard and protecting him. And to do that he needed Amy.

They'd go to the party, leave and there'd be nothing to worry about. Nothing to worry about at all.

CHAPTER SIX

'OUT? Why do we have to go out?' Amy asked, curled up in the corner of the sofa. 'I'm reading.'

Hugh took the novel out of her slackened fingers and placed it on the low coffee-table. 'Because I've got nothing to do.'

He could have added that he couldn't cope any longer with the distracting sight of Amy snuggled on his sofa, feet tucked beneath her and her hair rumpled—but he didn't. He'd worked out strategies to manage her presence in his office but his home was different. After just a few days he was beginning to get used to her being there. To miss her if she wasn't.

And it was beginning to make him angry. He didn't really understand why. Maybe there wasn't a why, he thought as she looked up at him. Or perhaps it was just this combination of liking and lust he couldn't get used to. Before Amy every woman had fitted neatly into one camp or the other.

'Where do you want to go?'

'The theatre?'

Amy hesitated for a fraction of a second. 'To see what?'

'Oh, I don't know. Let's just get out of here.'

'Okay.' She unwound herself from the sofa. 'Do I need to get changed or will I be all right like this?'

Hugh looked at the blue cotton dress that showed off her tiny waist and fabulous legs and swallowed. He turned away to pick up his wallet from the mantelpiece where he'd left it. 'You look fine. If you take too long we'll be too late to get in anywhere.'

'I'll just get my bag, then.'

With a swish of her skirt she left. Hugh jerked an agitated hand through his hair. He wasn't comfortable feeling like this. Not about *Amy*.

She'd been around since he'd first become Seb's friend, on the periphery of his life, but he'd never really noticed her before. He hadn't noticed the nervous habit she had of chewing her bottom lip, or the way she curled up to read anything and everything. He hadn't known she was obsessed with crosswords and hated plain chocolate. Strange things. Nothing particularly significant in themselves, but put together he knew they meant he was becoming fascinated about Amy. Who she was. In a way that was quite new for him.

And it scared him.

Because Amy wasn't someone he could rip out of his life if she got too close. She was in the fabric of it, woven in as tightly as if she were family. Whatever that meant. She was almost the little sister he'd never had—and yet the way he felt about her wasn't fraternal.

'Let's go, then,' Amy said as she reappeared, shoes on her bare feet and a tiny blue handbag hanging by her side. 'Are we walking?'

'We might as well.'

They stepped out onto the tree-lined London street. It was still bright sunshine but that oppressive, heavy heat had gone and a gentle breeze cooled the air. After the stickiness of the day it was so lovely to feel energised again.

Amy suddenly realised she felt happy. It had been such a long time since she'd felt like that. All the difficulties and complications of her life seemed such a long way away. She glanced across at Hugh. Being with him was quite remarkable too. It was almost like stepping through a dream. She'd never seriously imagined there'd be a day when he'd casually suggest they spend an evening together, just the two of them.

'Shall we try and see *Les Misérables* or would you prefer a more serious play?'

She wrinkled up her nose as she considered it. 'You know, I think I'd rather wander for a bit. I can't face sitting with a load of people tonight. It's too hot.' She cast a teasing glance across at him. 'And you can guarantee I'd get a seat with a tall man sitting in front of me. It always happens when I go to the theatre.'

The corners of his mouth quirked up at the edges and then that hard-to-resist glint coloured his eyes. 'Come on, then. Let's head towards the Thames. We can walk along the river.'

It almost felt like a date. Amy caught herself up on the thought. She mustn't let herself think like that. As far as Hugh was concerned she was Seb's kid sister. Someone he didn't have to make an effort for and could relax with. She had to be careful to have no illusions.

Hugh was kind. He'd always been kind to her, thoughtful in a way her brothers had never been. And that made him dangerous. It would be so easy to misconstrue that.

'Have you thought any more about your plans? When Barbara comes back?' Hugh asked, breaking the silence.

'Not really. I meant to ring round some agencies. Try and get some more temporary work, but I haven't.'

'There's still time.'

'Yes.' Another week. Barbara was away for just one more week. Saturday—tomorrow—was the retirement party. After that Sonya would be out of the country and by the time she returned Barbara would be back in post to shield him. Hugh wouldn't have any use for her any more. It would all be over.

It was odd how much she was enjoying being in Hugh's world. She'd never have believed it possible. So many of the preconceptions she had had about him were wrong. For one he worked extremely hard. The mountains of paperwork he created had her fingers flying over the keyboard and her shoulders aching by lunch-time.

And he was a much quieter man than she'd imagined. More serious. More intellectual. So why did he pick women like Calantha?

Over the past few years she'd only really seen him at parties with some blonde attachment in tow. He was always the centre of attention, flirtatious and witty. She hadn't really expected the boy he'd been to be so evident in the man he'd become. He still read a newspaper from the front to the back, still held political opinions that would have her father jumping up and down in fury, still bought organic food and opposed cruelty to animals.

So why Calantha? A woman whose thought processes didn't go further than who'd been at what party and had worn what. She bit down on the edge of her lip. Did she dare ask him?

'Hugh?'

He turned to look at her, impossibly handsome as ever, and she bottled out. It was none of her business anyway. 'Do you want to get some chips?' She pointed at a street stall.

'Rather than go to a wine bar?'

'We could sit by the river. Watch the boats.'

'If that's what you want.' Hugh turned and walked towards the stand. The smell of hot fat and vinegar filled the air.

Moments later he handed Amy a cone filled with fat, crisp chips. 'Thank you.'

'Do you want ketchup?'

'No.' She shook her head and bit into a burningly hot chip. This was about as perfect as an evening could get. She didn't have to be anything she wasn't, she had no responsibilities, no worries—and she was with Hugh. 'Everyone talks about newspapers being tomorrow's chip paper, but it's not true, is it?'

'What?' Hugh looked down at her.

'They don't use newspaper any more. Just this silly white paper that lets the grease through,' she said, spearing another chip with the small wooden fork.

He smiled. 'It probably breaks some EU regulation.'

'Probably.'

'You're a very cheap date.'

Amy looked up and her stomach flipped over at the mischievous glint in his blue eyes. He really was impossibly gorgeous.

'A bag of chips and a walk by the river.'

She looked away quickly. 'But then this isn't a date, is it?'

'No.'

'D-do you miss Calantha?' She risked another glance across at him. He was looking out across the Thames, staring blindly towards the Millennium Bridge.

'Callie? Miss her? No.'

Amy frowned. He sounded as though the question had been a strange one and yet until this Monday they'd been a couple. Been on holiday to the Maldives. 'You must do a little. You were together for months. And she's very beautiful.'

Hugh swung round to look at her. 'I didn't love her so I'm not missing her. Not all of us are like you, Amy. We don't all hope for love everlasting. We settle for the pleasure of the moment. It's a practical way of living.'

She'd never imagined Hugh could sound so bitter. His words sounded cold and cruel. It shocked her. 'You can't believe that.'

'Why not?'

His eyes challenged her to come up with a good answer, but she couldn't think of one. Not one she could put into a cohesive argument anyway.

Amy wandered over to one of the benches and sat down, with a small frown crinkling her forehead. If asked she'd have described him as an idealist, so why did he want to settle for less than was perfect? What she knew of Hugh and what he was saying didn't sit true—although it was no doubt an accurate description of how he was choosing to live his life.

Hugh sat beside her. 'You look worried. Your psychology degree is showing.'

'I'm sorry,' Amy said, forcing a smile.

'Don't be. Callie's stunning to look at and she wasn't looking for more than I could give her.'

'That isn't true, though, is it?' Amy said, her attention apparently on the chip she was trying to spear. 'Calantha wanted an engagement ring. She *did* want more than you're prepared to give.'

He shrugged. 'I think Callie wanted the security of my money more than anything else.'

Amy stared at him open-mouthed. 'That's a horrible thing to say. Why go out with someone you think so little of?'

'It's safer.'

'Than?'

'The alternative.' He stood up and threw his empty chip

papers into a nearby bin. 'Love is controlling, confining. I don't believe in the happy family façade. Look at Richard. It's making a fool of him.'

Amy threw the last of her chips away. 'It's not like that for everyone.'

'Not everyone,' he agreed. 'Sometimes it's worse.'

She looked at him curiously. It was as though the façade he presented to the world was cracking. Hugh was angry. Angry about something she didn't understand. Surely she was the one who should be carrying all the baggage of being brought up with parents who argued incessantly? Hugh's parents had been devoted. Excessively so. His father had resented having to share his wife with anyone, even his son—and his mother had over-compensated for that. In her eyes Hugh was perfect. 'So what do you believe in?'

'Passion.' He shrugged. 'Mutual need. Certainly not love.'

It was a stark statement. It made Amy feel unutterably sad. What had happened to Hugh to make him feel like this? Didn't he ever want to know the security of being loved, of having children, of making a future with someone?

'Even after everything I've seen...with Mum and Dad...I still believe it's possible to marry for life and be happy.'

'I bet you still believe in the tooth fairy too.' He stood up and walked over to the railings.

Amy let a group of Japanese tourists walk past before she joined him. Her fingers curved around the cool metal. 'Leastways, I couldn't live like you do. As though nothing matters.'

He looked down at her and she wondered what he was thinking. 'I suppose not.'

'I'd never want my children to experience what I did.' She glanced across at him, uncertain whether to continue or not. She'd never really spoken about how she felt. It was too personal. Even disloyal to her mum. She'd been so private.

Hugh reached out and gently stroked her cheek. 'Was it tough?'

His eyes were compassionate, thoughtful. 'Did you know my grandad, Mum's dad, was always playing away from home?' she began in a rush. His mouth moved in a negative. 'You'd have thought she'd have known better than to marry my dad, wouldn't you? But she did. And it was exactly the same. She couldn't change him any more than her mum could change her dad. And in the end he left us. Left her,' she amended.

'It wasn't his first affair?' he asked quietly.

'No. Mum used to find notes in his pockets or he'd be away on "business" for days. I can't remember a time when it wasn't like that. She used to get so depressed.' Amy brushed a tear away angrily. 'Hasn't Seb told you all this?'

'No.'

Hugh put his arm around her and pulled her into him. She listened to the sound of his breathing—and the stillness.

Why had she told him that? Was it because she wanted him to understand why he couldn't live like that? How much it hurt people?

How much it hurt *her*?

Did she hope he'd suddenly say he understood and wanted a long, committed relationship with someone like her? How pitiful was that? There must be something in her genes that predisposed her to want the wrong man.

She let go of the railing and turned around to rest her

back against it. 'What about you? Surely you want more than affairs? Don't you want children some day?'

'No.'

Amy was surprised. 'Ever?'

His reply was unequivocal. 'No. Too much responsibility. Too much chance of messing them up as our parents have messed us up. What's the point?'

'But your mum adores you. Why——?'

'And my father hated me.'

'Why?'

'Does it matter after all this time? He's been dead for years. The fact is, he did.'

Amy swallowed as she took in the bleakness of his words and recognised he was speaking the truth. Scenes flashed through her head and fell into place. They made a picture that showed her a different reality. Hugh's reality.

Hugh's father had been a stern disciplinarian; a man who'd always seemed to find his exceptionally gifted son wanting. She could remember her own mother's comments on the subject.

'He hated me probably as much as I hated him.' He glanced down at her. 'Are you shocked?'

'I knew he was too strict, but I always thought you'd managed to get through all that without it bothering you.'

He gave a hard bark of a laugh. 'How likely was that?'

Amy shook her head. 'Not very, I suppose. It's odd how much baggage you carry from childhood.'

Even Hugh, she thought silently. He'd always seemed to brush it off with a careless shrug, succeeding in spite of anything his father did or said.

It was *so* sad.

Hugh put an arm lightly around her shoulders as though what she was feeling had communicated itself to him. 'This is a very depressing conversation.'

'Isn't it!' She smiled swiftly up at him and then looked down at the dark, murky water of the Thames. 'Imagine what this place looked like a hundred years ago,' she remarked, making an effort to change the subject. 'It must have been such a busy, dirty place. Now it's all cleaned up with a designer bridge.'

'I like it. I like the dramatic sweep of the wings. They could so easily have gone for some mock-historical monstrosity.' His mouth quirked into a half-smile. 'I don't understand why all the benches face the Millennium Bridge and away from St Paul's Cathedral though.'

'Do they?' Amy swung round to look. 'They do! That's amazing. Why did they do that?'

'Whoever made the decision obviously prefers the new to the old.'

'I think that's terrible!'

His eyes smiled down at her. 'I thought you might.'

'It's ridiculous.'

'You don't have to convince me,' he protested, holding up his hands.

Amy let her natural laughter bubble up. 'Well, it is.'

They wandered back across the bridge and sauntered back the way they'd come. The conversation was light and apparently carefree, but Amy couldn't rid herself of the feeling of overwhelming sorrow.

Hugh. The man who appeared to have everything—but didn't.

She flicked a glance across at him. She had her answer as to why he chose women like Calantha. He didn't want a relationship that made him feel vulnerable, and loving someone was all about being vulnerable.

No one understood that better than her. She'd had a ringside seat. Despite everything, her mother had loved her father until the day she'd died. It was why he'd had the power to hurt her, why she'd taken him back time after time until he'd finally decided he didn't want her at all.

Loving was a risk. Knowing that had made Amy cautious and her experience with Greg had made her nervous, but it hadn't destroyed her hope for the future. It had tarnished it, but not destroyed it. Perhaps she was more resilient than she'd thought.

'What are you thinking about?' Hugh asked suddenly.

Amy swung her handbag loosely in her hand. 'All kinds of things. Me, mostly. I was thinking I'm like that character in *The Tenant of Wildfell Hall*.' He looked blankly. 'The one by Anne Brontë.'

He pulled out a long-forgotten thought. 'Credited as being the first feminist novel?'

'I'm impressed you know that.'

'Put it down to my expensive education.'

She cast a sideways glance up at him. 'I wasn't thinking of that, though. I was thinking of Helen. I think she's called Helen. It's a long time since I read it. Anyway, the main character in that had a truly horrible first marriage. And then she finds love. She describes a second marriage as "the triumph of hope over experience". That's like me, really. After my childhood I shouldn't want anything to do with love, should I?'

'I'd say, unreservedly, no. Better to go for eccentricity and the keeping of cats.'

She smiled. 'But I'm made of sterner stuff than that. Instead of giving up on it completely I've decided to pick carefully—using my head, not my hormones.'

He gave a crack of laughter. 'Good plan.'

'I think so.'

But that meant she had to stop dreaming of Hugh. And if she were honest she had to admit she did. He would never change. For whatever reason, he liked his life the way it was and it was never going to be right for her. Picking Hugh would be all hormones and no head at all...

Hugh couldn't stop thinking about what Amy had said. Or to be more accurate—the way she'd said it. With such determination in her voice. Such optimism in the face of reality.

In the adjoining office he could hear Amy moving about, humming softly to herself. He threw his newspaper to one side and pushed his leather chair back from the desk. It was as though she'd held a mirror up to his life and shown him a reflection he didn't like.

And yet what was the alternative? He couldn't pretend he didn't believe love was a destructive emotion. He couldn't tell her why; he couldn't tell anyone. It wasn't his secret to share. That belonged to his mother.

'Any chance of a coffee?' he called.

Amy opened the door connecting them, as he'd known she would. He'd called her more because he wanted to see her than because he wanted a drink.

'You're the boss,' she said, tucking one side of her shiny bobbed hair behind an ear, 'but Sonya's in the building. Are you sure you want me to go?'

'Perhaps not.' He stood up and stared blindly out of the window.

He heard her walk further into the room. A small silence and then, 'Are you all right?'

He spun round. 'Of course. Why shouldn't I be?'

Amy's dark eyes were full of questions. 'No reason.' She turned to go and then stopped. 'Are you worried about tomorrow? The party?'

He forced a smile. 'A little. I'll be glad when it's over.'

'So will I.' She perched on the edge of his desk companionably, ready to talk. He couldn't imagine Barbara ever doing such a thing. 'I bought a dress. It's silk and hideously expensive. Just think—if this charade went on too long I'd bankrupt you.'

He watched the way she crossed her legs. She had tiny, tiny ankles. Why had he never noticed that before? If he'd thought about it he should have known they would be like that. Her wrists were finely boned too. Sexy.

Pulling his eyes away, he muttered, 'Don't you have any work to do?'

'Plenty—but according to health and safety regulations it's not good for me to sit at a computer screen for too long without a break.'

'You've always got an answer, haven't you? If you were my permanent secretary I'd sack you.'

Amy chuckled, completely unfazed. 'I know you love me really,' she shot back. Something in him twisted. She was teasing him. He knew it. It was how they talked to each other. Always had done. But now he was aware of the impenetrable barrier she kept between them.

Amy wanted different things in life from him. She'd reluctantly agreed to play the part of his girlfriend, but in real life she wouldn't consider him a possibility. Because he wasn't. A man like him would only hurt someone like her. She knew that even if she didn't know why.

'Don't you want to know about my dress?'

He sat back down in his chair and picked up his pen. Some day she was going to find a man who could give her what she wanted. They'd buy a rose-covered cottage and live the perfect life with their two children. It was what he'd rejected so long ago so why did it now seem so appealing? 'Go on, then.'

'It's brown. The colour of melted chocolate with cream stirred in.'

'Sounds lovely.'

Amy laughed and slid off the table. 'You're horrid—but I don't care. I'm going to look lovely. The woman in the shop said I should always wear continuous blocks of colour, as it will make me look longer. And high heels to give me height and shape my legs.' She paused at the doorway. 'Actually, I think that works.'

So did he. The door closed and Hugh sat back in his chair. It was her tiny ankles that really did it for him. He was sure he could wrap one hand round them and meet at the back. Then he could slide his hand up the full length of her leg and past her hips to the tiny waist and small, jutting mounds of her breasts.

She was an elfin beauty and he'd never noticed. But what was really irking him was that she wasn't noticing him *at all*. Not by so much of a flicker of an eyelid could he detect she thought of him as anything other than Seb's friend. She was blithely keeping her side of their agreement while he was beginning to suffer. And although he knew he shouldn't want anything different, that was something that had started to bother him.

There was a faint tap on the connecting door before Amy put her head round it. 'Hugh, I've just been asked to take some figures over to Richard's office. If Sonya's heard that she'll know you're on your own.'

He raked his hand through his hair. Just one more day to get through. Just one more, he told himself.

'What do you want me to do?' she prompted.

He looked across at her. 'You'll have to lock me in here. Take the key with you.'

Amy looked doubtful. 'What if there's a fire?'

'Then you'll have to run along the corridor and let me out. If Sonya comes here I'll keep quiet and pretend I'm not here. There's not much else I can do.'

It was such a ridiculous situation to be in. Hugh heard the outer door shut and the sound of the lock turning.

CHAPTER SEVEN

THE dress had cost a fortune.

For one night! It seemed criminal, particularly when Amy thought about the money she owed. But what the heck? Even Calantha wouldn't have scorned to wear the soft caramel silk dress and for one night where was the harm in playing Cinderella?

Hovering near the surface, however, was an awareness that she was playing with fire. It made her feel euphoric and terrified at the same time. But it wouldn't do.

Hugh wouldn't risk letting anyone close and she wasn't prepared to accept anything less. Even so, she'd chosen a dress she hoped would be as distracting as possible. She told herself there was no harm in it. Not for one night.

'Ready?' Hugh's voice echoed up the stairs.

Amy shrugged at her image in the mirror. This was it. Tonight she was Hugh's girlfriend. She picked up her evening bag and let herself out of her bedroom. He was standing, immaculate in a dinner-jacket, at the bottom of the stairs waiting for her. She had to remember this moment. As an awkward adolescent she could never have imagined there'd be a moment like this one.

'Will I do?' she asked, walking towards him, careful not to catch the hem of her dress on her heels. 'Fine feathers...'

'Make fine birds,' he finished for her.

He seemed unusually nervous. She could understand that. Sonya in her own home would be more dangerous than anywhere else. It was lovely of him to want to protect

Richard so much. She slipped her hand into his. 'Do you think Sonya's really expecting you to arrive with me?'

'Why wouldn't she?'

'Well, it's possible she might not have believed you're really involved with me.'

He slipped his arm around her waist and kissed her lightly on her hair. 'Then it's up to us to convince her.'

She looked up at him, expecting to see a teasing glint in his mesmerising blue eyes, but he appeared quite serious. He was trying to remind her how important this evening was for him. She only hoped she didn't let him down.

'I'll do my best.'

He led her out to the hallway. 'I've parked the car at the front.'

The feel of his fingers at her waist was sending shivers down her spine. The movement of the silk between her skin and him made it feel more sensual, more erotic. Every impulse was prompting her to turn into him to tempt him into holding her close.

Dear God, what would it be like to kiss him? He had such a firm, sensual mouth. She had heard Imogen, one of his long-forgotten girlfriends, describe him as a fantastic kisser. It would be lovely to know what it felt like to be kissed by him. She'd said he was a great lover too. How would it feel...?

She pulled away and made a show of looking in the ornate hall mirror. 'How long do you think we'll need to stay?'

'Who knows?'

He sounded almost irritated. She bit her lip nervously. 'I hope no one asks where Calantha is.'

Hugh led the way down the steps and stood on the pavement. 'No one would be as rude as to ask you. If they talk about us they'll do it out of our hearing.'

'I suppose so,' she agreed as he opened the car door. She settled herself in the passenger seat and moments later he sat beside her. Amy glanced across at his handsome profile. It was unbelievable to think people would be gossiping about her and *Hugh*. Probably wondering what he was doing with someone like her. 'That's worse, though, isn't it?'

His blue eyes flicked a question.

'People talking behind your back. We've got no way of knowing what they're saying.'

He put the car into first gear and, with a quick glance over his shoulder, eased out of the tight parking space. 'Most of the time it probably wouldn't be worth hearing. Why are you so worried anyway?'

'Pride,' she answered swiftly. 'I don't want everyone saying, "She's much shorter than his usual girlfriends. I wonder why he's dumped Calantha? She was so beautiful. Much better than this one".'

His stern mouth softened into a smile. His head twisted round to glance down at her. 'You're an idiot. You know that?'

She looked at him questioningly as his sexy blue eyes sparkled with laughter.

'You're presupposing everyone liked Callie?'

'Didn't they?'

The laughter deepened. 'Did Seb?'

Amy looked down at her lap and then out of the window as the London streets passed in a blur. 'Is it a long way?'

'Haven't you been to Richard's new home?'

She shook her head. 'I've not seen much of him at all since he married Sonya.'

'I suppose not. It's about forty minutes from here,' he replied, his long fingers slipping the car into second gear as they approached a roundabout. 'Maybe longer if the traffic's bad.'

Amy let him drive in silence and Hugh made no effort to break it. No doubt he was thinking about Sonya—and about Richard.

She was thinking about him. It was so hard not to be seduced by everything he was. Hard to remember how being involved with a man like Hugh would break her.

Eventually they turned off a dual carriageway into a village that was a mixture of timber-framed cottages and stone houses. Within seconds he'd swung the car through wide wrought-iron gates and up a long gravelled driveway. Amy's stomach began to churn at the thought of what lay ahead of her.

They rounded a bend and Amy had her first glimpse of the Laithwaites' home. 'It's beautiful,' she breathed softly.

'It was,' Hugh said dryly. 'Sonya's made some improvements, which aren't doing a lot for the place. The marble bathroom has to be seen to be believed.'

'Why does Richard let her?'

He reversed his car neatly into a space between a Ferrari and a Bentley before answering. 'I think he senses he's got an unhappy wife and wants to keep the peace. Maybe he just adores her.'

Amy said nothing. She merely looked up at the Elizabethan house with its mellow bricks. Huge fire torches had been placed either side of the impressive doorway and the sound of soft music wafted out in the summer air.

'Let's go,' he said, holding open the car door.

She swung her legs out and allowed him to help her out. She stood millimetres from him, only the door between them. Her breath caught in her throat.

'You look incredible. Have I told you that?'

Amy couldn't look away. His eyes pinned her as securely as if his arms had held her still. She could see him
swallow a couple of times, feel him breathe. There was no
mistaking it. He did want her. On a purely physical level
he desired her. Blood pounded in her ears and she felt a
sense of exhilarating power.

'So do you,' she said, trying to lighten the atmosphere
between them.

His mouth quirked. 'I know you don't want to be
here…but I am grateful.'

'I don't mind—'

He moved quickly to place a finger across her lips. 'Let
me say it, Amy. Thank you.'

His fingers were warm. As he moved them away she
could still feel where they'd rested. She nervously fiddled
with the narrow strap of her dress and then, stepping away
from the car, smoothed down her skirt. 'You're welcome.'

She heard the car door slam and felt him move up behind her. 'Ready?'

Amy glanced across. 'Operation Deflect Sonya begin,'
she said buoyantly, her smile slipping slightly as his hand
reached for hers. 'I feel like a special agent.'

Together they began to walk over the gravel path, her feet
scrunching against the small stones and her heels burying
deep. Her ankle buckled and she let out a small cry of
pain.

'Can you manage?'

Amy lifted the front edge of her long skirt and pulled a
wry face. 'Tricky business this, being elegant.'

He gave a small laugh at the base of his throat and she
suddenly found herself spun into the air. She let out a small
shriek, grabbing tightly around his neck.

'What are you doing?'

'Helping,' he replied, settling her in a comfortable position with his arm beneath her knees and the other supporting her back.

'Put me down! People are starting to look.'

Carelessly Hugh glanced round at the handful of people who were also making their way towards the entrance. 'Who cares?'

'I do. You might drop me.'

He snorted derisively. 'No danger of that. You're such a midget.'

His arms tightened their hold and Amy was almost certain he'd lightly kissed the top of her hair. She couldn't be certain because it had been such a fleeting contact. Why had he done that?

With outward resignation she gave up protesting and let him carry her over the gravel. Her fingers felt the pulse in his neck beating and slid down the front of his jacket as he lowered her onto the stone step.

'Safe,' he whispered.

'Yes.' Her heart was thumping and she was sure her face was flushed. 'Thank you.'

She let her hand fall to her side, her eyes firmly on the middle button of Hugh's dinner-jacket. She didn't dare look up at him. She didn't want him to see how much his antics had affected her.

'Amy.'

She spun round in time to see Richard Laithwaite crossing the oak floor towards them. He reached out to kiss her on the cheek. 'I'm so glad you could come. And Hugh.' He reached out to grip the other man's hand in a firm handshake. 'Glad you're here. You'll find most people have already gone out to the marquee.'

Richard turned back to Amy and smiled. 'You look enchanting.'

'Thank you,' she replied, with a look down at the rich silk of her dress.

'A definite look of your mother, if I may say so.' He looked over his shoulder as Sonya wafted through the door at the far side. She was instantly visible. Her red hair hung loose in soft curls and her periwinkle-blue dress was cut low across her amazing cleavage.

Amy cast an anxious glance up at Hugh.

'Sonya, do you remember my god-daughter?' Richard asked, drawing his wife into the conversation.

Unbelievably Sonya smiled and held out her hand. 'Amelia Mitchell. Of course I do, darling,' she said, laying a gentle hand on her husband's jacket. 'Although I must say you don't resemble the photograph Richie has of you in his study.'

'She was only a little girl then.'

'And now she's grown up and beautiful. Your dress is stunning. You must tell me where you found it.' She turned her blue eyes on Hugh. 'And, Hugh, how lovely to see you again. You've become quite a stranger.'

Amy watched, mesmerised, as Sonya floated across to kiss his cheek. Her whole body seemed to be part of her welcome as she pressed up close against him. Then she pulled away, unnecessarily rubbing his cheek with her fingers. 'I've left a lipstick mark on you. Your little Amy will never forgive you if she catches sight of it.'

Amy forced a smile.

Sonya swung round and linked her arm with her husband. 'Don't you think they make an enchanting couple?'

Richard's eyes looked from one to the other. 'A couple? Are you and Amy—?'

Hugh thrust his hands deep into his pockets and cut in. 'It took a great deal of persuasion.'

Richard's eyes crinkled at the edges. 'So that's why

she's helping you out in the office with Barbara away! And what does Seb make of this development?' he asked, casting a humorous look up at his friend before breaking off, a look of pain passing across his face.

'Are you all right?' Hugh asked, stepping forward quickly.

The older man nodded, pushing his hand firmly in the centre of his chest. 'Fine. Absolutely fine. It's a touch of indigestion. That's all.' As the pain eased he looked at Hugh and winked. 'I'm on enough tablets to make sure it isn't anything else.'

'But—'

'It's nothing,' he said more firmly than he'd intended. At least it appeared so as he followed it by a firm grasp on Hugh's arm and a much softer, 'Enjoy the party.'

'Everyone's here. It's going to be a beautiful party.' Sonya gently stroked Richard's lapel. 'You know, darling, I think I ought to check on our guests. I'll walk over to the marquee while you greet people here. You ought to stay in the warm.' She didn't wait for her husband to reply. 'Hugh. Amelia,' she said in goodbye and then swept her exit.

Amy was staggered. How could Sonya *do* that? If she hadn't held the purple mesh underwear in her hand and seen Sonya spilling out of her jacket in Hugh's office she'd have found it difficult to believe Richard's wife wasn't devoted to him. She glanced across at Hugh and wondered what he was thinking. Didn't he long to tell his friend what his wife was like?

'Sonya's worked hard to make this evening a success,' Richard said quietly.

Hugh put an arm around Amy. 'I'm sure it will be an excellent party.'

'Yes. Yes, so am I,' the older man said, turning back to

look at them. 'Now, you must take Amy and get her something to drink. I have to say hello to my other guests.' He
reached across and gave Amy another kiss on the cheek.
'It's lovely to have you here.'

'Are you sure—?' she began, but he didn't let her finish.

'Perfectly. Go on, you two. Enjoy the party.'

Hugh ushered her forwards and Amy heard Richard's
booming voice talking to the couple who'd been hovering
behind them. Her heels clicked on the wooden floor and
candlelight illuminated in soft shadows the character of the
house. Next to her Hugh reached out and took her hand.
She felt a sudden jolt as his fingers curved around hers.
She rushed into speech to cover her embarrassment. 'How
could she do that?'

'Shh,' he cautioned.

Amy checked over her shoulder. Richard was happily
engrossed in another conversation. 'He doesn't look well
tonight.'

'He isn't.'

'He looks so tired.'

'That's what this is all about. He's not well at all and
Sonya knows it.'

She turned back. 'He didn't look so ill on Monday. I
hadn't expected…' She hadn't expected him to look like
that. So grey. So pained. No wonder Hugh wanted to protect him. Anyone would.

Hugh led her through the door to the left and she discovered the source of the music. A small group of musi-
cians sat in the far corner of a large room with no furniture
in it but full of couples dancing. Amy glanced about her.
She could feel eyes turn to look at her, almost hear the
whisper of a question pass around the room. 'Do you want
to go outside?' she asked quietly.

'No.'

She looked up at him.

'Let's dance?'

Dance? Stay in this room? With people talking about her? Watching her?

With Hugh's arms around her?

It was as though he were moving in slow motion, Amy thought as Hugh came towards her. She didn't move. She stood, not breathing, as he turned to face her. His free hand came to hold her waist and he lifted the hand he was holding to rest against his chest. Slowly, rhythmically, they began to move together.

She'd never considered dancing to be erotic—but she'd been wrong. She could feel every line of his body, sense the way he'd move and turn. It felt so right, so perfect to be in his arms it made her feel frightened. It felt as if she'd come home. That with Hugh she'd found somewhere safe.

But it wasn't safe.

Was this how her mother had felt when she'd realised she loved her father? This feeling of inevitability, of being sucked in by a strong magnet she was powerless to resist. It felt as if her whole life had been leading up to this moment and she could do nothing about it.

His fingers splayed out on the soft silk of her back. His arms held her securely as he spun her round.

A moth to a candle. If she'd been hurt by Greg, how much more would she be by Hugh—a man she loved?

Loved?

Amy closed her eyes and breathed in the soft, musky scent of his aftershave. *Loved.* How could this be happening to her? When had it come? She'd recognised the danger and been on her guard every moment. Hadn't she? Her heart seemed to beat in time to the music. Her body swayed against his, her hand cradled inside his much larger one.

It wasn't possible. Not with the man who'd once told her there were 'so many women, so little time'.

But it wasn't that man she'd fallen in love with. She loved the man who listened to her as though what she was saying mattered. The man who cared enough about his friend to put this charade together in the first place. The man who visited his mother even though he hated her constant chatter and muddled way of talking. The man who was hurting from the rejection of his childhood...

The man she understood.

Hugh was many things. Good and bad. She knew about them all. She knew because she'd watched him. Since she'd been a young girl she'd taken a special interest in him. She knew the names of all his girlfriends because it had mattered to her. She'd teased him and scolded him for the same reason.

She loved him. Had always loved him.

Like breathing in and out, it would always be a part of her life. She would always love him. There was nothing she could do about it.

His fingers moved on her back and it felt as if she'd just taken a drop on a roller-coaster.

And if she wanted him, she could have him.

For a time.

No woman had ever held his attention for long. He would tire of her. He would never want to hurt her, but it would be inevitable. When the time came for him to move on to a new and more fascinating woman she would be left broken.

She knew it. History was repeating itself. Only this time it would be her sitting at the kitchen table sobbing. Her waiting for him to come back home, long after it was plain to everyone else he wouldn't.

The only thing she had to decide now was whether that was a price she was prepared to pay.

She lifted her head from his chest. 'He believed us, though, didn't he?'

'Who?' Hugh's voice sounded blurred, mellow, as though he were being called back from somewhere far away.

'Richard. He didn't seem to question us being together. I thought he might.'

Hugh spun her round. 'Why?'

'Because you've never shown the slightest interest in me,' she returned steadily. The knowledge smarted. It was only now—now she had beautiful clothes and an elegant haircut. Before that she'd blended in with the wallpaper.

'If I'd ever made a play for you Seb would have killed me.'

'That wouldn't have stopped you. If you'd wanted to.'

The grip on his hand tightened and his voice was low. 'You were hiding.'

She stepped back, although she couldn't go far because of his hand about her waist. 'Of course I wasn't.'

'I think you were. For some reason you didn't want anyone to see how beautiful you were. You've deliberately taken a backstage role and done everything you can to escape notice.'

'That's not true,' she gasped.

'You never believe any of the compliments people pay you.' He reached out and pushed her swinging bobbed hair back from her face. 'Why are you so negative about yourself?'

'I do. I...'

His arm pulled her in closer. Her eyes were on his and her fingers splayed against his chest. 'Relax.'

'It's difficult.'

He felt a tremor run through her. His fingers absent-mindedly soothed, gently caressing her cheekbone with his thumb. He could feel himself becoming mesmerised by her eyes. They were the deepest brown with tiny flecks of gold and they spoke of a vulnerability, some deep hurt he wanted to understand. He wanted...

He wanted to kiss her. Slowly, very slowly, he lowered his head.

That first kiss was tentative, but he felt the response shiver through her. 'You're beautiful,' he breathed softly against her mouth before closing in on her trembling lips. He knew the exact moment she relaxed against him. Melted. He let his hand trail back into her silky soft hair and cradle her head.

Dimly he became aware of her tensing beneath him. Gone was the compliant Amy. She smiled up at him. 'I don't know what that was supposed to prove except that you do kiss very nicely.'

'I what?'

'Kiss very well. I suppose it's because you've had a lot of practice over the years.'

'Amy,' he began dangerously.

'Shh, someone might hear you.' She pulled away. 'You were very convincing, that's all. Let's go outside.'

Hugh couldn't remember that ever having happened to him before. It confused him. *She* confused him. He let her walk away from him.

She'd changed—and it wasn't just the clothes. Although that was quite a dramatic difference. The soft caramel colour of the silk dress she was wearing did something special to her skin. The way the fabric swirled around her legs was sexy. *She* was sexy. It wasn't the clothes. It was her. He wanted to peel the silk away from her body and explore what she was hiding beneath it. He wanted...

He caught himself up on a breath. He liked her—and if he took these feelings any further he would end up hurting her.

At the door she'd paused, turning back to look at him. Her expression was a mixture of understanding and laughter. Perhaps she could read what was going on inside his head? Was that a good thing? Or a bad one?

'I can't see anything of Sonya; she's disappeared,' Amy remarked as he joined her. 'But I can see several people from work. Adrian Dunn is over by the arch and I'm sure I recognise the man he's talking to.'

'Peter Wray,' he answered after a cursory glance.

Amy scarcely heard him. Her stomach flipped unpleasantly and then the bottom of it disappeared altogether.

'Amy?'

Hugh's voice at her elbow was almost a distraction as she made eye contact with a sandy-haired man in his mid-twenties.

'What is it?'

'It's a *who*,' she said between closed teeth, 'and it's my past.'

Gregory bounded up the two shallow steps and crossed the terrace towards her. 'Amy? Is that you? I scarcely recognised you.'

'Hello, Greg,' she said in a voice that sounded empty.

Hugh moved across to stand next to Amy and extended his hand. 'Greg...?'

'Hinchman,' she finished for him. 'You met at Christmas.'

'Ah, yes. I remember.' Hugh wrapped his arms around her. She was perfectly aware of what he was doing. Grateful even. Amy relaxed back into the warmth of his body, but her fingers gave his forearm a gentle nip as a warning not to overdo it.

Then she looked back at Greg, beginning to enjoy the expression of stupefaction on his face. He kept looking at her and then up at Hugh. She'd almost forgotten the effect of her new clothes, the contrast she now presented to the Amy he'd known—and dumped. It simply didn't matter any more. She smiled. 'Are you living in London now?'

'Y-yes. Yes, I am. I'm in Putney. You? I thought you were staying in Manchester.'

Hugh let his fingers trail down the side of her neck. It was as much as she could do not to close her eyes and whimper. 'I changed her plans.'

Greg was watching them closely. 'Oh, I see,' he said nervously.

He looked so much smaller. So much more youthful and lacking presence than he did in her imagination. It was incredible to believe this colourless man could have inflicted such pain. He'd made her feel worthless. For a while.

Greg put his hands awkwardly in his trouser pockets. 'Where are you working?'

She hesitated. The truth was hardly going to impress. Then she jumped at the sound of Hugh's voice. 'Amy's delaying starting anything permanent until after we get back from the States next month.'

Amy could have laughed out loud at the expression on Greg's face. It was a moment to treasure and the small circles Hugh was tracing in the hollow between her neck and collar-bone only added to it. 'There doesn't seem to be any rush,' she agreed with a quick glance up at Hugh. His eyes twinkled down at her and she felt an answering gleam in her own. Dimly she heard Greg asking her a question. 'I'm sorry?'

He looked more acutely uncomfortable. 'I was just asking what part of the States you're going to.'

'Houston,' Hugh answered for her.

Greg shuffled his feet slightly. 'Are...are you...' his hand made a waving gesture from one to the other '...are you...?'

At last Hugh took pity on him. 'Together?'

Greg's Adam's apple bobbled alarmingly, but he managed a nod.

'Didn't we say? Richard has our address if you need to contact Amy about anything.'

Greg's face was an absolute picture of humiliation, puzzlement and embarrassment. Amy turned her face into Hugh, trying to stifle a laugh.

'Now, if you'll excuse us...Greg, we need to go.'

Immediately he stepped backwards. 'Yes, yes, of course.'

Still she couldn't speak, but she smiled and nodded. Hugh's hand gently propelled her down the steps and out across the lawn before laughter overcame her.

Hugh leant on the stone wall. 'Whatever did you see in that—?'

'Don't say it!' Amy forestalled him, breaking into renewed laughter.

'I can't believe you let that idiot hurt you. He's even worse than I remembered.'

Amy wiped at her eyes. 'Has my mascara run?'

'No,' he said, tilting her face up to look. 'You're still beautiful.'

She felt as though the air were contracting around her. He sounded as if he actually meant it. *Beautiful*. Hugh Balfour thought she was beautiful. At this precise moment she *felt* beautiful.

Not insignificant. Not the poor, little thing whom Greg

Hinchman had betrayed then dumped. But beautiful. It was an intoxicating feeling. She wasn't going to fight it any more. She was going to enjoy it. For one evening. She was going to enjoy being the centre of Hugh's attention, the woman other women looked at and thought lucky.

Her mouth twitched into a smile. 'Thank you for saying all that to Greg.'

'It was nothing.' He walked down a step before turning back to ask, 'How did you feel seeing him again?'

'Fine.' Amazingly fine, Amy thought on a bubble of laughter. She shouldn't feel so fine. Why wasn't there some residual regret? Some feeling of anger, even, at the thought of how publicly he'd dumped her. But there was nothing.

'I'm glad.' His fingers gently pushed the swinging hair away from her face.

Amy felt as though she'd lost the capacity to breathe. Greg had never made her feel like this.

'You deserve someone much better than that,' he said softly.

'Yes, I do.' And for the first time she really believed it. Standing on the step above him, for the first time she could look directly into his eyes. They were warm. Questioning.

He was going to kiss her again and she wasn't going to resist him. She was going to let whatever happened happen—without fear. She was going...

Her eyes closed as his mouth met hers. Softly. Temptingly. His hand cradled the back of her head.

He was so good at this, she thought. Each tiny flick of his tongue sent shivers shooting round her body, licking warmth across her veins.

'Amy.' His voice breathed her name rather than spoke it. It made her want to laugh and cry at the same time. Her fingers crept across his shoulder and up his neck into the back of his hair. It was thick and springy to her touch.

He wasn't play-acting any more than she was. This was real. He might not love her, but he had finally noticed her as a desirable woman.

And she was stupid, after all. Instead of turning and running in the opposite direction as fast as she could, she was staying. She was letting him seduce her into believing she had no alternative.

CHAPTER EIGHT

DIMLY she heard Richard's gruff voice say Hugh's name. He lifted his head and rested his forehead on hers, his fingers still wreathed in her hair. 'You aren't what I expected,' he said softly.

Amy smiled. She had nothing to say. He was everything she'd expected.

Richard's voice called again. 'Hugh?' He shuffled round the corner, his hand pressed firmly in the centre of his chest. 'This heartburn is getting worse. I'm going to sit in the library.'

Amy saw the pain etched on his face and looked questioningly at Hugh. He knew more about her godfather's condition than she did. Surely this couldn't be heartburn.

'I'll come with you,' he said, moving swiftly to support the older man. 'We both will.'

'Of course.' Amy nodded even as her godfather shook his head.

'I don't want a fuss. I was wondering if you'd seen Sonya?'

Hugh's mouth became a firm, hard line. 'Do you need her?'

'Just to tell her where I am. Nothing to worry about.'

'I'll find her for you.' He glanced back at Amy. 'Do you want Amy to go with you?'

'I want you to stop fussing. It's nothing.' He rubbed at his chest. 'Just tell Sonya if you see her.'

'I'd be happier if—'

Richard cut him off. 'Take Amy to the marquee and get

her something to eat,' he said, patting her on the shoulder. 'It's lovely to see you again, my dear. I'll come and find you and we'll have a good chat later.'

Amy smiled, unsure what else to do. 'I'll look forward to that.'

'Don't believe a word of it. I saw you two earlier. You must wish me a mile away.'

'He shouldn't be on his own,' Amy remarked softly, watching him shuffle back towards the house.

'No,' he said, reaching for her hand. 'I never thought I'd say this, but let's find Sonya.'

She felt his fingers slide down her bare arm and they interlaced with hers. It was an innocent enough gesture but it trailed fire, sparks shooting through the rest of her body. She cast a swift look up at him, trying to see if he was aware of the impact of his touch. His face was bland enough. Teasing. She looked down at their hands. 'What's this about?'

His grin widened. 'If we're going to find Sonya, you've got to look after me.'

'You baby,' she retorted, feeling her own face respond with a smile. They began to walk along the gravel path towards the marquee, past the huge rhododendron bushes.

She felt ridiculously happy and it had everything to do with Hugh. Her stomach was whirling as if several hundred butterflies had been let loose inside her and her mind was concentrating on not allowing a ridiculous grin to stay pasted on her face. She hurried to think of something vaguely sensible to say. 'I know about Richard's angina from Dad. It's just I didn't expect him to look so…drawn, I suppose. I thought angina was okay once you were on the tablets.'

'I don't know much about it either,' Hugh replied as they approached the entrance to the marquee.

Inside was a crush of people. Small huddles of people were standing in almost every available space. Several people in their near vicinity looked round and smiled or waved a welcome at Hugh. It had to be Hugh because she didn't recognise anyone. 'Do you know all these people?' she whispered.

'Pretty much, to some degree or another. I can't see Sonya, though.' Hugh let go of her hand and passed her in front of him, letting his hands trail across her shoulders. He pulled her tightly into his frame. 'Keep close to me. I don't want to end up having to search for both of you.'

'I'm not going anywhere,' she managed, unnerved by the feel of his body pulled up tight against hers.

'We're going to have to see if she's the other side of the marquee. Failing that, I suppose we'll have to look round the garden. I don't like the idea of Richard on his own up at the house.'

'No.'

Hugh kept her close as his eyes scanned the crowd. They made some headway towards the centre of the marquee, but there was no sign of Sonya.

'Hugh!' He turned at the sound of a man's voice calling his name. 'I've been looking out for you.'

Amy stood back a little as a tall man, slightly balding, gripped Hugh's hand in both of his. 'I've not seen you since...I don't know when. Must have been a good three years or so.'

Hugh pulled his gaze away from his search and concentrated on the man clutching at his hand. 'Peter...Clayton.'

'Clayton. That's it,' he confirmed, noticing the slight hesitation.

'It's good to see you again,' Hugh said smoothly, his hand reaching for Amy's. 'Have you seen Sonya Laithwaite? She's wanted up at the house.'

'I have.' Peter turned back towards his companions. 'Did you see where Sonya went?'

There was a small discussion in which there was no clear outcome. 'Not to worry,' Hugh interrupted. 'If you see her, tell her Richard is waiting in the library.'

Hugh kept hold of Amy's hand and they pushed their way through the crowded marquee. 'Where can she be?' he muttered. 'She must be in the gardens somewhere.'

'Try that way,' she offered, pointing at the path leading directly towards the woodland.

'It's as good as any other.'

They followed the twisting path. With every step Amy could sense Hugh's urgency. After a short way the path opened out on a small clearing surrounded by beautifully tended flowerbeds. There were a number of people gathered there, mainly sitting in small seating arrangements listening to the string quartet. They skirted around the edge.

'Sonya's not here,' Amy said after a quick glance round. 'Maybe she went back to the house?'

'Perhaps. If we take the path round by the croquet lawn we can check out the area by the swimming pool and tennis court.'

'She's not likely to be there.'

'I can't see her here,' Hugh said unarguably. 'The whole garden is open to guests. She could be anywhere.'

'I suppose.' She shuffled her feet.

Hugh looked down at the high stilettos. 'Can you manage in those or do you want me to come back for you?'

'I'll manage. I don't like the thought of Richard back at the house on his own.'

'We'd better try and make it look like a casual stroll. Richard wouldn't forgive me if I worried his guests. He's been playing down his angina since it was first diagnosed.'

They began to walk up the small incline. 'You're really worried about him, aren't you?' Amy asked.

'Of course. He's pushed himself to stay in control of Harpur-Laithwaite. He shouldn't have done it. I can manage it. I won't let him down.'

Amy smiled. The tone of voice he used when talking about Harpur-Laithwaite was very similar to Richard's. Despite having agreed to join Richard for a trial period and very reluctantly, it had clearly become something of a passion. 'I'm sure he doesn't doubt that. You know, you two are very similar. You've really grown to love it. That's amazing considering how reluctant you were to accept Richard's offer in the beginning.'

Hugh looked down at her with a strange expression in his face, but he said nothing.

Amy followed slightly behind him, still connected by the linked fingers. His expression was curious. Almost as though he was going to say something to her but had decided not to. It probably wasn't important and they had to find Sonya.

The light was beginning to fail and the solar lighting placed around the gardens was beginning to come into effect. Practically they lit the way and the shadows they cast over the paths were eerie and romantic.

At the top of the path it forked in two directions. 'Which way now?' Amy asked breathlessly.

Hugh looked around, trying to get his bearings. 'I think left.'

She glanced back the way they'd come. The marquee looked smaller and glaringly white in the middle of so much green. Beyond it the mellow brick of the Laithwaites' Tudor home looked magical. 'You can see what attracted Sonya, can't you?'

Hugh's face hardened. 'Come on. Let's see if she went

this way. We'd better get back to the house and check on Richard ourselves if we don't find her.'

They walked steadily round past the spinney and back towards the house. Amy stumbled slightly and Hugh steadied her. 'I'm sorry about this, Amy. Not much further, I promise.'

'What's the building behind there?' Amy asked, pointing behind some large bushes.

'The swimming complex. There's a barbecue area and some changing facilities.'

'Do you want to check there?'

Hugh shrugged. 'No point. There's no one round here.'

Amy walked past him. 'We may as well. At least then we can be certain she isn't up here.'

Hugh followed behind her. The swimming complex Hugh'd so carelessly referred to was more glamorous than she'd expected. It was a separate building, for a start, covered with glass and with big double doors all along one side. It was completely quiet and although she rattled one of the handles it didn't open.

'It's all locked up. Let's go back down to Richard.'

Amy held up a finger. 'Listen. I think I heard something.'

They both stood still for a moment and concentrated. Above the faint rustle of the evening breeze there was silence. 'You're right. Let's get back and check on Richard.'

Hugh caught her arm. 'No, you were right. There is someone. Round the back. I heard laughter.' He strode out. 'Hello. Is anyone here?'

'Where are we going?' Amy asked, following.

'There's a door to the changing rooms back here.' He turned the handle and it swung open. 'Sonya? Are you here?' Hugh walked through and switched on the light.

The lobby was empty and the changing cubicles also appeared deserted.

'There's no one here,' Amy said, shivering suddenly.

'Then the door shouldn't be open. I'll check by the pool.'

Amy followed closely behind him. Initially she'd have said it was empty too, but as her eyes became adjusted to the dimness she sensed movement. She touched his arm but he'd seen more than her, his eyes adjusting more quickly to the dark.

'Sonya.' His voice startled her as it dripped with contempt.

Amy squinted at the couple spread out on the floor. She heard the sharp expletive the man let out and watched them sit up and look round at them. They seemed to move in slow motion while she stood by helplessly watching. In the end Sonya let out a gentle laugh. 'Oops.'

Hugh didn't register having heard it. 'I'm glad we've found you, Sonya. Richard's having some kind of trouble with his angina. He asked us to find you and tell you he's in the library.'

Sonya uncurled herself from the tiled floor and wandered carelessly over to the lounger where her evening dress had been thrown.

Amy had to admit her body was fantastic. She could easily have posed for one of those men's magazines on the top row of the newsagents if she'd wanted to. She certainly had the confidence. 'I may be a few moments.'

He nodded curtly. 'Amy and I will go and reassure Richard you'll be joining him shortly.'

'I didn't notice the little brown mouse behind you,' Sonya said, stepping into her red dress.

Hugh almost pushed Amy back through the door and out through the lobby to the path outside. 'Let's go.

There's no point standing about any more. She'll be better if she doesn't have an audience to play to.'

'I don't believe that. Doesn't anything embarrass her?'

'I doubt it.'

Amy frowned. 'But a couple of days ago she was undressing in your office. That's why I'm here.'

'You said it yourself. She obviously finds the danger exciting. As far as her marriage with Richard is concerned, there's no one more dangerous than me, no one closer than me.'

He was walking quickly until he suddenly remembered Amy and slowed his pace. He waited until she joined him. His hands fitted around her face. 'She makes me feel so sick. She's a foul woman.'

Amy stood still. There was real anger in his voice, mingled with pain and desperation. She'd never observed that in him before. 'I'm glad you're with me,' he said softly, easing the soft fall of dark hair away from her face. 'You're so different. So very lovely.'

Slowly, very slowly, he lowered his face to hers until their lips touched. It felt almost reverent, certainly cleansing, as though he was putting something beautiful over something hideous. Amy immediately felt an overwhelming need to comfort him. She wrapped her arms tightly around him and held him. Quietly. Not really understanding what he was feeling, but content to give him what she could.

At last he pulled away and rubbed his thumb over her lips. 'We'd better get back to Richard.'

She let him take her hand and they walked in silence back down the path. His face was a mask and Amy made a conscious decision not to ask him any questions, although she desperately wanted to know whether he was going to say anything to Richard about what they'd seen.

As they approached the house from the main lawn a middle-aged lady in a black dress began running towards them.

Hugh let Amy's hand drop and asked urgently, 'What is it, Laura?'

She answered on a hiccup, 'Oh, Dr Balfour, Mr Laithwaite is having some kind of heart attack—'

'Where? Is he still in the library?' he asked, cutting her off sharply.

'Yes, sir.'

'Have you rung for an ambulance?'

Under his quick-fire questions the woman gradually began to calm. 'About three minutes ago. Mr Laithwaite appears to know what to do himself. He's used some kind of spray under his tongue already.'

'Excellent.'

'We haven't been able to find Mrs Laithwaite.'

Hugh's face hardened. 'Don't worry about that. Mrs Laithwaite will be here directly. If you wait and tell her what has happened when she arrives, Amy and I will see to Richard.'

He didn't wait for her this time. He walked rapidly, his long strides purposeful. Amy followed a little fearfully. Apart from television dramas she had never seen anyone having a heart attack and had very little confidence she'd be able to do anything useful.

In the library there was very little activity. Richard was sitting up in a chair. His face was grey, presumably with pain, and his hand was bunched in the centre of his chest. He was breathing heavily, concentrating on it. But he was calm.

Amy walked quietly over. 'Do you want me to do anything?'

Richard tried to acknowledge her presence and gave a

ghost of a smile before an expression of pain passed over his face. Amy laid a gentle hand on his grey hair and looked at Hugh kneeling beside his friend. 'What can I do?'

Hugh looked up, his blue eyes more fearful than she'd ever seen them before. 'Will you make sure someone is looking out for the ambulance at the gates? They need to be open with someone there to direct them up the drive. Get someone else to wait at the front door to lead the paramedics through to the library.'

Amy nodded. She went quickly out of the library. She didn't know the house at all, but there seemed to be any number of staff waiting around nervously. There hadn't been anyone who'd thought of waiting for the ambulance crew. Amy issued Hugh's instructions and watched gratefully as Richard's staff ran to carry them out.

A flash of red alerted her to Sonya's return. She turned back from the main entrance as Sonya approached. There was no concern on the redhead's face. Her expression was one of irritation, as though she thought her husband's sudden ill health was something he'd arranged expressly to irritate her. Amy felt her contempt for the other woman deepen.

'Is he still in the library?' she asked curtly.

Amy nodded. 'With Hugh. Yes.'

'How touching.' Sonya turned towards the library, stopping momentarily to ask, 'Why's the front door open?'

'We're waiting for the ambulance.'

Sonya clicked her tongue. 'Shut it for now. Anyone could walk in. I'm sure there'll be someone capable of opening a door when they get here.'

Amy ignored her and left the door wide open, even pulling a chair across to ensure it stayed that way. Then she followed Sonya back to the library. The transformation in

Richard's wife was extraordinary. It was as if someone had waved a magic wand over her. She oozed concern and sympathy. Her red-tipped nails stroked back his grey hair as her voice crooned, 'The ambulance will soon be here, darling.'

Amy's hands itched to rip those red talons away from her godfather. Bile gathered in her throat as she watched Sonya's hateful parody of concern. Then she turned to look at Hugh, expecting to see his eyes blazing with anger. His lips had tightened into a harsh, disapproving line, but he calmly stepped back to give up his place to Sonya.

Amy wanted to shout at him, make him do something about Sonya. An almost imperceptible shake of his head held her silent as he came to stand next to her. He leant down and whispered, 'Is there someone at the gate?'

She nodded.

'Good. It's a difficult turning to see in the dark and the light is fading fast.'

Richard groaned as another spasm of pain hit him. 'Hugh?'

'I'm here,' he said, stepping forward.

'Look after everything, will you?'

'I'll explain what happened,' Hugh said quietly, taking hold of the other man's flailing hand.

Richard shook his head. 'Just…just let it go on. It'll be easier.'

Hugh laid a calming hand on his shoulder.

'You and Amy…stay over.'

'Just leave it to me.'

'I'm sorry, Hugh,' he mumbled finally, pushing at his chest. 'So sorry.'

There was no question as to the moment the paramedics arrived at the house. They were calm and professional, but the people around them scurried and spoke in overloud voices.

Amy sunk back towards the wall and watched as two men asked questions in calm, sensible voices. Sonya hovered decorously, but at the centre of it all was Hugh. It was Hugh who answered the questions. Hugh who held open the door as Richard was carried out, his oxygen mask in place.

Amy remained quiet, trying to keep out of the way, just grateful to see how much calmer Richard looked now professional help had arrived. She sank to the floor and sat patiently until Hugh returned.

'Has the ambulance gone?'

'With Richard and Sonya in it.' Hugh nodded. 'You did well.'

'You did! I didn't do anything.'

Hugh smiled and pulled her up from the floor. 'You did what I asked you to do quietly. That's more than can be said for anyone else. Are you ready for the next part of your duties?'

'What's that?'

'We've got to finish off this party.' Hugh glanced down at his watch. 'There's fireworks in about an hour and then we've got to take care of the guests staying over.'

'But won't they go home when they know what's happened?'

'I doubt it,' Hugh said, picking up his jacket. 'It's late and some of them have come a long way.'

'Even so—'

'Richard has plenty of staff to look after them. It won't be too difficult. All we have to do is to make sure they don't feel uncomfortable about sticking to their original plans. Ah, Laura,' he said as the woman in the black dress put her head round the door, 'Amy and I are going to take over as hosts. Would you make up a room for us?'

'Of course, Dr Balfour. Is Mr Laithwaite…' She broke off with an agitated wave of her hand.

Hugh put an arm around Amy. 'He'd done all the right things, apparently. The paramedic I spoke to seemed quietly confident.'

'Well, that's a relief,' she said with a tight smile.

'Laura, let me introduce you to Amy. This is Amelia Mitchell, Richard's god-daughter.' He looked down at Amy. 'And this is Laura Brundle, Richard's housekeeper. I don't think you've visited here since Laura arrived.'

Amy smiled. 'It's nice to meet you.'

The housekeeper nodded her head in a brisk fashion and said, 'I'll put you and Dr Balfour in the room he stayed in last time he was here.'

Amy started to speak, but Hugh forestalled her with a quick, 'Thank you.'

'And I'll make a list of where I've placed everyone else,' Laura Brundle continued. 'There are just seven guests who intended to stay the night and their rooms are ready for them.'

'Excellent.'

Amy's head was whirring. *One room.* Just *one.* She'd distinctly heard Richard's housekeeper say she was putting them in a room together. She knew she ought to protest, to tell him it wasn't possible, that he was wrong to assume so much just because she'd let him kiss her. And yet…

Hugh's arm stayed firmly around her, his fingers resting against her bare shoulder. If he slept with her it would just be for comfort; she knew that. He didn't love her. Not as she did him. Not in that all-encompassing, overwhelming way she did him. She believed he liked her. Perhaps that was enough.

For one night.

She couldn't fool herself it would be any more.

And then what?

As the housekeeper shut the door of the library Amy turned within the circle of his arm. 'Why don't I just get a taxi back to your house and you can manage everything here? It's not as though I know anyone.'

Hugh sighed and rubbed an agitated hand across his tired eyes. 'Because at some point during the night Sonya will be coming back to the house and if you're not here I'm going to be in trouble.'

'Not now,' she protested. 'Not after what we saw by the swimming pool.'

'You don't know Sonya. Now she'll be angry and she'll want to punish me. If I'm staying in this house overnight I need you to be with me. It's no use you being along the corridor.' He walked back outside the library.

Amy hesitated, completely torn by her desire to give in and her desire for survival. She ought to protest. Tell him it wasn't possible. He looked back at her through the open doorway and he smiled at her standing in the centre of the room. The corners of his mouth tilted, but his usual laughter didn't touch his eyes. 'We're just going to share a room.'

She swallowed. He sounded as though he meant it and perversely it wasn't what she wanted to hear. 'Just share?'

Hugh walked back into the room and took hold of her hand, carefully linking his fingers through hers. 'Just share. You can put cushions down the centre of the bed if it'll make you feel more comfortable.'

'I don't have anything to wear,' she whispered, wanting to protest, but completely confused as to what she wanted to object to. Was it being forced to share a room with him? Or was it his not wanting to make love to her?

Had she been the only one who'd been affected by their kiss? Had she been wrong when she'd thought he'd begun to be attracted to her? She'd never thought it would last, but she had hoped...

'Come on, Amy,' he said as he studied her face. 'It's not that bad. Worry about it later.'

That was easy for him to say, but impossible for her to do. He really didn't know what he was asking.

'We probably ought to circulate,' Hugh said sensibly. 'I don't know how many people will have seen the ambulance...'

She pulled away. 'Are you going to make an announcement? About Richard?'

'No.'

As they walked out onto the terrace Amy thought she'd never seen Hugh looking so tired. Twice she thought he might have been about to say something to her, but each time he changed his mind. Of course, it might have been nothing important, but Amy sensed he'd been about to confide in her—and then decided not to.

A small group of people clustered near the water fountain and looked up as they passed. 'Did you see the ambulance?' one began.

Amy felt Hugh sigh rather than actually heard it. He was finding this difficult. She supposed that wasn't surprising. He'd worked with Richard for years and had known him all his life.

With a quick glance up at him, she stepped forward with her best society smile. She could take the pressure off him by answering these questions. 'Richard has been taken unwell. He was adamant it shouldn't spoil the party, and Sonya's with him, of course.'

The small murmur of sympathy was broken by a woman in her fifties exclaiming, 'Amelia Mitchell. I didn't recognise you for a moment. I haven't seen you for…what must it be now, darling?' she asked, turning towards her florid-looking husband.

He shook his head and puffed out his cheeks. 'Don't know. Must be two years. I haven't seen your father for well over a year. How is the old man?'

Amy kept her smile pinned to her face as she belatedly recognised an old friend of her father. 'Both he and Lynda are well.'

'Good. Good. And your mother?'

His wife laid a restraining hand on his arm. 'She died, George. Don't you remember? We sent flowers.'

Hugh placed an arm around Amy. 'If you'll excuse us? Richard asked Amy and I to take Sonya and his place this evening.'

Amid the general acquiescence a lady in blue murmured, 'She must be Hugh's new girlfriend. I thought he was seeing a model.'

'That was before. He's seeing a designer.'

Beside her Amy could feel Hugh's body tense. 'Let's go, Hugh. Have a good evening.' She smiled.

'I'm sorry,' he began as she led him through the trelliswork and back up towards the marquee. 'Meeting someone who knows your father was what you were worried about.'

'It was inevitable,' Amy replied. 'It doesn't matter. You know, I think we should split up. We can cover much more ground that way.'

He nodded.

'You take the marquee, I'll go back to the house,' she suggested. 'When will we hear any more about Richard?'

Hugh brushed a hand across his face. 'Later. I'll phone later. It'll take a while before they will know any news to tell me.'

'It'll…I'm sure it'll be all right,' Amy offered.

Swiftly Hugh reached down and kissed her. 'Let's hope so. Are you sure you'll be okay on your own?'

'Fine.'

He gave her a swift smile and walked towards the marquee as she'd suggested. Amy watched him go for a moment before turning back towards the house. This Hugh was a man she hardly recognised. Something was going on here she really didn't understand at all.

CHAPTER NINE

HUGH shut the door of the bedroom with a bang that ech-oed round the room. Amy jumped nervously. 'Have you phoned the hospital? Is there any news?'

'Richard's comfortable,' he said with a tight smile, lines of sheer exhaustion showing on his handsome face. 'We can expect Sonya back some time in the next couple of hours.'

'Oh,' was all she could think of replying. It was inad-equate, she knew it was, but what else could she say?

'Everyone seems to be settled comfortably into their rooms. I think we're probably safe now until the morning.' He sat on the side of the bed and took off his shoes. 'We'd better get to bed.'

Amy stood awkwardly, her nervous fingers pleating the silk fabric of her dress. 'Have you got any ideas about what I'm going to sleep in?'

He looked up at her. 'I can't magically create anything. Open the cupboards. Is anything there you can use?'

Tentatively she opened a couple of drawers, but there was nothing except a small lavender sachet. 'No.'

'You'll have to make the best of it. It's only one night. Even if I wanted to ravish you, Amy, I honestly don't have the energy tonight so try and relax.'

She felt foolish. Her fingers curled around the mahogany knob of the chest of drawers. *How embarrassing.* She was behaving like a nervous teenager. Instead she was with her brother's best friend who obviously didn't think of her in that way.

144

Reluctantly she turned round. He'd thrown his jacket over a nearby chair and had begun to unbutton his shirt. She'd never imagined she'd be in Hugh's bedroom while he undressed. It felt impossibly intimate. She'd seen Hugh in swimming shorts dozens of times over the years, but this felt so different. To her it felt sexual.

He might be too tired to think of doing anything—but the exhaustion tugging at her eyelids wasn't having the same effect on her. She could all too easily imagine what it would be like to run her hands over his muscular chest, feel the small dark curls curling there. Amy closed her eyes to shut out the images filling her head.

'I'm so tired it hurts. What an evening.'

Amy opened her eyes in time to see him pull down his trousers over lean hips. She licked her lips nervously and hastily looked away. They were just sharing a room. That was all. The bed was wide. Hugh would, no doubt, be asleep almost before his head hit the pillow.

But she wouldn't...

She felt completely tied in knots by her emotions. What she wanted. What she didn't want. What *he* wanted. Amy looked desperately out of the window. *What he didn't want.*

Amy sat on the opposite side of the bed and undid the ankle straps of her sandals. The difficulty was all in her head. They were just sharing. *Easy.* He would go to sleep and so would she.

But what if she talked in her sleep? What if she told him she loved him? What if she rolled over because her subconscious knew how much she wanted to be near him? Slowly she slipped off her shoes.

And Hugh didn't know how little she was wearing under this dress. She hadn't bothered with a bra. She'd so little to support it hadn't seemed worth the expense of buying

a different bra that wouldn't have straps across the back.
And as for knickers—it was a tiny scrap of lace. No more.
She couldn't lie next to him like that.

Unless…

'I've got an idea—' she began.

'If it involves me sleeping in the bath,' he interrupted,
'I can tell you now, I'm not doing it.'

Her brown eyes flicked across at him and she smiled in
spite of the crippling embarrassment she was feeling. 'It's
not as bad as that. Look.' She pointed at the bottom sheet.
'I can sleep under the mattress cover and you sleep on
top.'

'What?'

'Then we can both sleep under the duvet.'

'You're serious?'

'Absolutely.' Amy nodded vigorously. 'I've got nothing
to wear in bed.'

'Does it matter?'

'It does to me.'

'Okay.' He shrugged, pulling back his side of duvet and
getting into bed. He lay, staring at the ceiling, with his
arms behind his head.

'Hugh!'

'What's the matter now?'

Amy looked at him disbelievingly. 'I've got to get ready
for bed and I can't do it with you watching.'

'I'll close my eyes.'

'No.' She wrapped her arms protectively round her
body. 'You've to turn your back.'

'Turn around?' Hugh gave a crack of laughter.

'What's funny?'

'I was just thinking about the contrast between you and
Sonya. I've got one woman who thinks the idea of sleeping

with me—sleeping in the same bed—is a fate worse than death and another who…well, who doesn't.'

Amy pulled back the mattress cover. 'Just turn around.'

Obediently he rolled over and lay so he faced the window. 'Tell me when you're done.'

Her fingers fumbled with the short side zip on her dress. 'Just keep looking away.'

Hugh heard the sound of her dress pooling on the floor and the desire to laugh left him. He kept his face turned towards the window and listened for the little sounds that told him what Amy was doing. He heard her pad across the bedroom floor and heard the bed creak as she climbed in.

'You can turn round now.'

He turned round. She was lying in the bed with the duvet pulled up tight against her chin. Her face, still with traces of her soft make-up on it, was looking nervously across at him. He smiled at her, as much to reassure himself as her.

'You'll need to turn out the light. There isn't a cord above the bed.'

He looked up. She was right. With a sigh he got out of bed and walked over to the door. One flick of the switch plunged the room into darkness. As he walked back to the bed he knocked his shin against something sharp and let out a low expletive.

'What was that?'

'Nothing. My leg just made contact with something hard.'

Hugh heard the springs as she moved and tugged an agitated hand through his hair. This was going to be impossible. 'Right.'

Gradually his eyes adjusted to the darkness. He could feel her tense as he climbed in beside her. She was lying flat on her back, her hands clutching at the sheet covering that separated them.

Amy smiled. 'It's awkward this, isn't it?'

'Not particularly,' he lied. He'd never been in a situation like this before. He'd never lain next to a semi-naked woman and not been able to stretch out his hand to touch her if he'd wanted to. And he'd never been with a woman he'd wanted to touch so much before.

They lay in silence so long he began to wonder whether she'd fallen asleep. 'Amy?'

'Hmm?'

'Nothing. I just wanted to know if you were asleep.'

'No.'

He turned over to lie on his side, facing her. In the dimness of the bedroom he could see her face. She looked so vulnerable, so perfect, with her wide dark eyes and sensitive mouth. He was in bed with *Amelia Mitchell*, Seb's sister. Beneath the thin sheet and duvet she was topless and that thought was playing havoc with his hormones.

He spoke in a conspiratorial whisper. It seemed to match the night, the darkness and the feeling of intimacy. 'Have you ever played Truth or Dare?'

'What's that?'

'You have to either answer my question truthfully or you must complete my dare.'

She pulled the duvet higher. 'It sounds risky.'

'No riskier than this.' He laughed and it echoed in the stillness. 'I wonder what Seb will make of us sharing a room.'

'It was your idea. I could easily have got a taxi.'

Hugh stretched out a hand and smoothed back her hair off her face. 'Not easily at this time of night.' He moved his fingers abstractedly across her forehead. Slowly.

Soothingly. 'What makes a woman behave like Sonya, do you think?'

Amy found it impossible to answer. The sensations shooting through her body, the feeling of closeness, paralysed her mind. The darkness wrapped itself around her and she lay quietly.

'Richard's a clever, astute man and yet he's completely taken in by her. He appears to adore her.'

'Yes.'

He didn't appear to notice she'd said anything. 'What makes a man hide the truth from himself like that?'

His voice radiated hurt. She could feel the pain pulsating through his fingers.

'I don't know. Why did my dad treat my mum like he did? And why was your dad so spiteful to you? People make bad choices, I suppose. If they thought about it they wouldn't do it.'

Hugh's hand stilled on her forehead. 'I know why he did that.'

'You do?' She raised herself on one elbow and her shiny hair swung in a curtain around her face. 'Why?'

Her face showed her amazement and Hugh felt an overwhelming need to tell her. Ever since his mother had told him he'd kept her secret. Perhaps he'd already guessed it and it hadn't been the shock it should have been. Maybe he was even glad.

'Because I wasn't his son.' In the end the words came easily. He'd never spoken them aloud before.

'Not...'

'His son,' Hugh finished for her. He watched a small frown appear in her forehead and reached up to smooth it away.

'D-do you...do you know that for sure? Did your mum say...?'

'After he'd died. I always knew he hated me.'

'But then who? I—I mean how?'

He felt his face relax into a smile. 'The usual way, I think.'

'Yes, but...' She let herself fall back down on the bed. *Hugh's mother.* It was inconceivable. She wasn't the sort of woman you'd ever believe would have an affair. She was mumsy, for want of a better word. She didn't seem to have a desire beyond her home, her garden and her son. 'But you were only ten when your dad died. Did she tell you then? Why?'

'I asked her.'

Amy's mouth moved soundlessly as she tried to formulate the questions she wanted to ask. If that had happened to her she would have thought the world had ended. 'How did you feel?'

'At the time I was relieved. It made sense I wasn't related to him. I felt nothing but dislike for him and it was so obviously shared. It was later, when I was older and really began to think about it, that the knowledge started to bite.'

His fingers moved gently to stroke her hair back from her face. She looked up into his blue eyes, glistening in the darkness. 'What happened? Do you know?'

'I know what she told me. She met my dad, for want of a better way of describing him, when she was seventeen and they married when she was eighteen. He was eleven years older than her.' Hugh sighed and rolled over on his back. 'He adored her, but then we both know that.'

He paused. Amy held her breath. How could you know someone so well and not know them? All this going on in Hugh's life and she hadn't had the faintest idea. 'Go on,' she prompted.

'They'd hoped to have children but after several years

they had to accept they probably wouldn't have any.' He reached across and pulled her towards him. 'Do you mind if I hold you?'

Did she mind? Every nerve in her body was pulsating with need of him. She'd take any excuse he offered to hold him. 'I don't mind,' she said, letting him move her body against his. As she snuggled up against him she could feel his breath on the top of her hair and the beat of his heart underneath her fingers. It felt comfortable. Right.

'Dad was offered a six-month contract in Hong Kong. It was while he was away that my mum met my father, my natural father.'

'Who was he?'

There was a slight pause before he answered. 'She won't tell me. Somehow, among them all, they made the decision to let me be brought up as I was.'

Hated by the man he'd thought was his father. It was all so *wrong*. 'Did he know about you? Your natural father?'

'Oh, yes.' Hugh's fingers played in the softness of her hair. 'It was all very carefully thought about. Mum went away to stay with her parents until after I was born. Everyone felt the most important thing was that there shouldn't be any gossip.'

Amy smiled against his chest. 'I can hear her saying it.'

'They managed the whole thing very well. No one suspected anything. When my dad returned from Hong Kong we moved back home and started playing happy families.'

'But why doesn't she tell you now?'

Hugh shifted Amy in the crook of his arm. 'She doesn't like to think about it. It was an unhappy time in her life and she prefers to pretend it didn't happen. Perhaps she even believes that now.'

'So you don't know?' He was silent and Amy turned within his arm to look up at him. 'Or do you?'

'I think I know,' he said at last.

Amy sat up, clutching the sheet to her chest. 'Who?'

She could see him deciding whether to tell her. See the thoughts flitting across his face. 'I think it's Richard,' he said at last.

'No!'

He shrugged. 'Perhaps not. No one's told me. It's all conjecture.'

'B-but…'

'It makes sense. I know.' He pulled her back down to lie beside her. 'And I think Sonya knows. Or at least suspects something.'

Small, insignificant events started to slot into place in Amy's mind. It was possible. It was more than possible.

But *Richard*? Hugh's father? Was it possible?

Nervously Amy chewed on her lower lip. *And Sonya?* Why would Sonya want to sleep with her husband's son?

'If I'm right I'm the most effective weapon Sonya has to hurt Richard with,' he said, answering her unspoken question. 'Richard's will treats me like a son. Sonya married him for his money and she's going to lose a huge chunk to me.'

'Have you never asked him?'

Amy felt him shake his head.

She understood so much without him having to say it. Just why they were so close. If Richard had died this evening Hugh would have lost his chance of speaking to his father about what had happened. *If* Richard was his father.

'You have to ask him,' she said quietly. 'Or your mum. One of them. You have to know.'

His arm tightened about her and he placed a soft kiss on the top of her head. 'Go to sleep, Amy.'

She lay still, not daring to move in case she disturbed him. Curved against the warmth of his body, she listened to his steady breathing knowing she would probably never feel as connected to another human soul again.

And she ached for him. Her imagination was all too ready to see the ten-year-old boy he must have been, desperately confused with no one to talk to. Having to grow to adulthood knowing you've been lied to by all the people you should be able to trust.

Amy moved her hand to rest on his chest, concentrating on the rise and fall it made with each breath. It was hardly surprising he'd decided to keep his relationships simple. Why he didn't want real intimacy. Why he didn't trust it.

The knowledge made her feel sick inside. She felt that same seeping sense of powerlessness, the certain knowledge she could do nothing to change it. In the quiet of the night she rolled over and pressed a kiss on his bare skin. It felt like goodbye.

Amy woke first.

Hugh's arm was heavy across her body. Warm, comforting and exciting. His skin was brushing against her skin. Every nerve ending in her body was screaming with awareness of him. It was almost a physical pain to want him so much.

In her dreams she would roll over and wake him with a kiss. She'd take his face between her hands and press her lips to his. Watch his eyes open and darken with desire. Then he'd gather her close and tell her that he loved her.

In her dreams.

It would never happen. The reality was completely different. He didn't love her. He didn't seem to love anyone. It was as though he'd shut love off as a possibility. He wanted to keep control of his emotions so nothing could hurt him again. She could understand that. With the logical part of her brain she could see how he'd reach that decision.

Her fingers stroked against the small hairs on his arm. But he was wrong. It meant he'd spend a lifetime alone.

People would come in and out of his life. For a few years he might not even notice he was lonely. Everyone liked him. He'd always be surrounded by friends, people who thought they knew him well. And there'd be women who'd be happy to sleep with him. Beautiful women whose bodies he'd enjoy. But that was where it would end. Ultimately he'd be alone.

Perhaps that didn't worry him? He'd been effectively alone all his life. It would take a very powerful love to make him risk trusting anyone with his emotions.

To trust *her*.

And that wasn't likely, was it?

If she kissed him, she might see his eyes darken with desire, but it wouldn't mean he loved her. It would mean he desired her. He might even make her his girlfriend for real. For a time.

Amy felt her eyes well up. A single tear inched over the edge and rolled down her cheek. It would be agony to be his lover and know he'd only given her his body. She wasn't the type of person who could live in the moment and let the future take care of itself. She wanted it all. She wanted the whole fairy tale. She wanted the 'happy ever after' ending. She wanted for ever.

And knowing that, nothing else would do.

She'd been granted a reprieve. Last night she would have let him make love to her, simply because she would have been powerless to resist. Now, in the cold light of day, she recognised what a huge mistake that would have been.

He had issues to face. She had to let him go. If he'd made love to her it would have been because he'd wanted physical comfort. This morning he would have regretted it. She was his best friend's sister. He didn't want to hurt her. Maybe he was already going to regret telling her so much, letting her see the real Hugh.

With her eyes on his sleeping face, Amy gently lifted his arm and rolled out the side of the bed. He scarcely stirred. Gently she reached out and stroked the bristles on his chin. She'd never seen him like this. It was a memory to treasure.

Hugh murmured in his sleep and she snatched her hand back. *What did she think she was doing?* The cold morning air feathered her skin and she became aware of just how little she was wearing. She wrapped her hands about her body and grabbed at her evening dress before scurrying to the *en suite* bathroom.

If he'd opened his eyes and seen that… *How toe-curlingly embarrassing that would have been.* There could have been no pretence then that she didn't love him. He would have seen it on her face. If he'd looked as far as her face.

Amy ran herself a deep bath, grimacing at the noise of the water on the enamel. It was time to make some decisions. Grown-up, gritty ones. She let the hot water soothe her, resting her head on the back and sinking down low.

First she needed a job. Any job. Then somewhere to live. She had to let go of her mother's house. Obvious, sensible things. Things she should have done months ago.

And, most importantly, she needed to let go of Hugh. She needed to make decisions on her own life without being aware of where he was, what he was doing and what he was thinking. Somehow he'd always been a factor with-

out her being aware of it. Perhaps he was even the reason
why she'd been so reluctant to sell the cottage in Henley?

'Amy?' Hugh called through the closed door. 'How long
have you been up?'

'I'll be out in a minute,' she called back.

'I'm going to use the bathroom down the corridor.'

'Okay.' Amy sunk down under the water. This was so
completely bizarre. Even sharing his home hadn't felt this
intimate.

Resurfacing, she hurriedly finished washing and then
dried herself on a white fluffy towel. She'd brought nothing with her, not even a toothbrush. It felt weird to be
putting her evening dress back on. Last night she'd felt
elegant, this morning she felt awkward.

One quick glance in the mirror showed her make-up had
largely sunk into her skin, but there was nothing she could
do about that. Pulling open the mirror-fronted cupboard,
she did find some toothpaste and rubbed some on her teeth
with her forefinger. Not brilliant, but the best she could
do.

This really was the morning after the night before. It
had all the awkwardness. She opened the door and lifted
her skirt off the ground to walk to the bed, sitting down
to do up the ankle straps on her high evening shoes.

'Are you ready for breakfast?' Hugh asked as he came
back into the bedroom. 'Laura seems to have everything
under control.'

He'd dressed already. It wasn't fair for any one individ-
ual to look that fantastic this early in the morning. His
shirt was open at the neck and she could see the dark hair
curling in the V. She knew it continued in a single line
down his abdomen. Amy turned away and forced her
thoughts into a different direction. Her fingers concentrated

on the final buckle. 'Have you telephoned the hospital this morning?'

'Yes. I've just rung.' She looked round as Hugh passed his hand across his unshaven chin she'd touched earlier. 'He passed a comfortable night.'

'That's good.'

'Yes.'

Their conversation felt strained and awkward. Was he regretting telling her so much about his private thoughts? For a man who avoided intimacy, he'd shared an enormous amount. Amy desperately wanted to tell him he could trust her, that she'd never betray his confidences. The words welled up inside her head but instead she stood up and smoothed down the caramel silk of her dress. 'Is Sonya up?'

'Not yet,' he replied, holding open the door. 'As soon as she leaves for the hospital I'll put you in a taxi.'

His words hit her like a blow. He wanted her to leave. That shouldn't have surprised her. Her eyes darted across to look at him. 'What about you? When are you leaving?'

'I'll follow when all the guests have gone home.'

'I could stay—'

'There's no need.'

'I suppose not.' She caught herself up. She wouldn't be needy. She'd made the decision to let him go. 'It'll be good to get some sensible clothes back on. This isn't great day wear.'

She went to walk through the door, but he stopped her with a gentle hand on her arm. 'Amy.'

Blinking hard, she managed, 'Yes?'

'Thank you for last night.'

She turned, forcing a smile. 'Anyone hearing that...'

Something of his usual glint coloured his eyes. 'Your reputation would be in tatters. One of Hugh's bimbos... I know. I've never told a soul before. Thank you for listening. I'm glad you were here.'

Hot tears pricked at the back of her eyes. She couldn't help herself—she reached out and stroked the side of his face. The bristles scraped her fingers. 'You're welcome.' And then she realised what she was doing, pulling back her hand awkwardly. 'Thank you for talking to me.'

It fell heavily by the side of her body and she turned away, embarrassed.

'I don't think anyone's up yet,' he said, as though the moment had never been.

'That's good.' Amy caught her lower lip between her teeth. She sounded like an idiot. She had to talk naturally. As they'd always been able to do before... Before she'd realised she was fighting a losing battle. Before she'd realised she loved him.

'Oh, I need my bag.' Gratefully she turned away to pick up her small evening bag from the bedroom chair. 'Let's hurry up and get downstairs. It'll be better if we're down before anyone else.'

'Yes,' he agreed.

The breakfast room was to the right of the kitchen and led out onto a wide terrace. It was a lovely room, although the ornate swags and tails at the window rather overpowered it. Sonya's touch, Amy thought critically.

'Laura's set everything out in here,' Hugh remarked as he opened the French doors. 'It's probably warm enough to eat outside. What do you think?'

The wrought-iron table and chairs on the York stone outside looked very inviting, particularly as they faced a two-hundred-year-old oak tree. Amy didn't have a chance to answer, though. Before her eyes Hugh's face changed. Her mouth started to form the question, What?

'You're up surprisingly early.' Amy spun round to see

Sonya standing in the doorway. 'I'd no idea we had a dress code for breakfast.'

Her beautiful face was impeccably made-up and her Titian hair curled softly around it. Honesty compelled Amy to admit Sonya Laithwaite was a stunning-looking woman, but her mouth was sulky and her eyes were hard. Amy couldn't help but wonder whether Hugh was right in thinking she suspected he was Richard's son.

She shivered as she thought about her draped across Hugh's desk. Why would she be so cruel?

'I've rung the hospital,' Hugh said, opening the last of the double doors.

Sonya lifted one bare shoulder and picked up a fruit salad from the sideboard. 'If there'd been a problem they'd have telephoned.'

'He's passed a comfortable night,' Hugh continued coldly. 'I told them you would be in first thing.'

The eyes flashed as she glanced back at him. Amy was stunned at the venom. 'Naturally.' She walked past Hugh and sat calmly on the terrace.

Through the open doors the soft smell of Old English roses punctured the air. It contrasted sharply with the tension between Hugh and Sonya. The air fizzled with hostility.

Amy walked over to the table and selected a glass of orange juice. 'You must be very worried,' she observed quietly, her back to Sonya.

'I'll live.'

Amy turned in time to see the redhead pierce a piece of pineapple. Her behaviour was mystifying. Hugh looked grim as he walked over to Sonya and sat opposite her. 'He's ill and he's old. If you do anything—'

'You'll what?' she challenged. She put down her spoon. 'He'll never believe you, Hugh. Tell him what you like.'

He leant forward, his eyes blazingly angry, but he spoke in a calm, measured voice. 'You may be surprised—'

'Hugh,' Amy interrupted. The sound of footsteps in the hallway meant she had to stop him. Sonya held his glance, dipping her head at the last moment. Then he glanced across at Amy. 'I think people are stirring.'

He followed her glance to the doorway and was in time to greet Colonel Lewis and his wife. 'Good morning.'

The colonel looked past him. 'Sonya, my dear, how is he?'

Two bright spots of colour burnt in her cheeks, but Sonya Laithwaite was charm personified. Miraculously her eyes welled up with tears. 'He's doing very well, but I must go to the hospital. I'm sure you understand.'

Amy watched in disbelief as she dabbed at her eyes. It was a performance worthy of an Oscar. She glanced across at Hugh. He could have been carved from granite for all the emotion he showed. He obviously expected no different from Sonya.

'Hugh and Amy will take care of you. I know you'll understand I need to be with my husband,' Sonya added, before walking briskly from the room.

'The poor girl,' Mrs Lewis said, watching her go. 'Such a sad thing to happen. Will Richard be all right?'

'So we understand.'

'And he's your godfather?' she wanted to know, turning to Amy.

'He's a friend of my parents. Do help yourself to breakfast.' Amy neatly drew their attention to the buffet table.

The next half an hour was fully taken up with Richard's guests. She scarcely had time to think. Everyone was very concerned for Richard and clearly didn't intend hanging around long after they'd eaten.

She was vaguely aware Hugh had slipped out of the room but didn't realise why until he leant down and whispered in her ear. 'I've arranged for a taxi to collect you at half past.'

'But Sonya—'

'Has already driven away in her sports car. Whether she'll go straight to the hospital or not, I don't know, but she's left.'

Amy looked round at the last of Richard's guests. 'I can stay if it will help.'

He was shaking his head even before she'd finished speaking. 'Go home. I'll ring you as soon as I have any news.'

There was no reason for her to stay. Amy glanced down at her wrist-watch. It was only two minutes before half past. 'I'll wait by the door.'

Hugh nodded briskly before his attention was claimed by the Radwell-Petersons. She picked up her handbag from the side-table she'd left it on and automatically checked for her key. Then she said her few goodbyes. Hugh didn't look up. He continued his conversation about irrigation.

Walking away physically hurt. She felt so involved, but to Hugh she was just another guest to manage. He had other things on his mind.

The grand entrance hall was completely deserted. She stood at the doorway watching for the taxi. As it wound its way up the long drive Amy looked back over her shoulder, hoping to catch sight of Hugh. There was no sign of him. He was busy and they'd said their goodbyes. She had to leave.

The journey back to London was swift. After the first few miles the taxi driver gave up any attempt at conversation. Amy watched the miles disappear in a browny-green blur and then shades of grey as they entered the city.

'This is it, love,' the driver remarked, pulling up outside Hugh's home.

His voice jerked her back to the present. 'I'll need to

go inside to get some money,' she began. 'I don't have enough—'

'No need,' he said over his shoulder. 'The gentleman back at the big house has got it covered.'

'Oh, right. Thank you,' she managed, opening the door and catching her heel on her evening dress. For the first time she became aware of what she was wearing. It didn't really matter what connotation the taxi driver put on her returning home in an evening dress, but she could feel her face becoming heated with embarrassment.

Awkwardly she climbed out of the car and stood for a moment looking up at Hugh's house while the taxi drove away. She'd give anything to be back with Hugh. To know what was happening—to him, to Richard. With a sigh she let herself into the house and tried to ignore the echoey silence.

It was the start of a long day. Every few minutes she found she was looking at the clock. Wondering. At lunchtime she made herself a light salad and ate it in quiet solitude. There was no news. Nothing. Not even a telephone call to tell her there was no news.

Amy looked at the clock again. It was barely fifteen minutes since she'd last looked. She idly picked out an apple from the fruit bowl and had eaten half of it before she realised she wasn't hungry. Irritated, she got up and threw the half-eaten fruit into the waste bin.

She cast another glance at the clock while she made a coffee. The minute-hand seemed frozen, it was moving so slowly. *If Hugh would only phone.*

But the small silver handset sat silently on the coffee-table, mocking her. She carried her coffee back into the conservatory and picked up a newspaper, flicking through to find the crossword. The temptation to ring Hugh on his mobile was almost overwhelming and yet she managed to resist it. If he wanted to talk to her, he would. It was as simple as that. Perhaps he had nothing to say?

She turned her attention back to the crossword and found she was doodling in the side margin rather than solving any of the cryptic clues. Throwing the paper to one side, she closed her eyes and let the emotions that had been building in her find relief in tears. She wasn't even entirely sure what she was crying for. It was all such a muddle.

By late afternoon her head was aching. Her eye sockets felt as though sharp needles were stabbing them and a dull thud pulsated in her temples. And still no news from Hugh. With weary acceptance she pulled a cushion across to rest on the arm of the sofa. Pulling her feet up, she lay down and closed her eyes against the building pain.

She woke suddenly to the sound of someone moving about the kitchen. Amy jerked up. 'Hugh?'

'No, dear,' said his mother. 'You were sleeping so peacefully I didn't like to wake you. Would you like a cup of tea?'

It seemed such an incongruous question Amy almost laughed. Moira Balfour was standing in Hugh's kitchen as though that were where she always was. Amy sat up and pulled the cushion onto her knee, hugging it close. 'I'd love a cup of tea.' And then, 'Have you heard from Hugh?'

'Not since this morning,' Moira replied, calmly pouring boiling water onto the tea-leaves and setting it to one side to brew.

Amy let that information sink in. She hadn't known Hugh had rung his mother. Had he rung from the hospital? And what had he told her exactly?

'Hugh doesn't have any proper cups,' she said, pulling a tea strainer out of her bag, 'so we'll have to make do with mugs.'

'I didn't realise he had any proper tea either.'

'I always bring it with me. His father never could abide the tea in the bags. Always said they were the sweepings off the floor.'

Amy wanted to say something. To protest that her husband wasn't Hugh's father. To break through the façade of perfection Moira Balfour presented. But she hadn't got the right to do that. It was almost as though the other woman had drawn a veil over that part of her life and, in her mind, it almost hadn't happened. Wasn't that what Hugh had said?

Moira poured the tea out with all her usual care. 'Biscuit?'

'No, thank you.'

'You look exhausted,' she said, coming round to join Amy in the conservatory.

Amy accepted the mug with a quiet murmur of thanks. All those times she'd sat in Moira's comfortable kitchen and listened to stories of Hugh's childhood she hadn't understood anything. 'I am tired. It's the shock, I suppose. Did Hugh tell you about Richard?' she asked, looking up.

'I thought he looked unwell the last time I saw him.'

If Hugh was Richard's son his mother was remarkably cool about it. 'Apparently he's had angina for a long while.' Amy sipped her tea, watching.

'Years,' Moira replied. 'Tell me how Hugh has been treating you.'

Amy let the conversation move away from Richard Laithwaite. Truthfully she was glad of the company. They talked about how Amy had got on at Harpur-Laithwaite, what she hoped to do when Barbara returned to the office, how Amy had enjoyed staying with Hugh and whether she thought he'd marry Calantha.

They ate pasta dressed in a light tomato sauce and played a long game of Scrabble, which Amy didn't win until nearly midnight. Moira sat back in her chair with the score-pad in her hand. 'I don't think you'd have won so easily if you hadn't managed to put "thespian" on a triple word score.'

'No,' Amy agreed with a slight smile. She'd been beating Moira at Scrabble since she was eighteen. The first summer after her mum's diagnosis had been such a hard one and Moira had been there for her. Quietly supportive. A shoulder to cry on and a ready provider of home-made cakes. And later, when her mum's condition had worsened, she'd been one of the few people who'd sit with her while Amy took an hour or two off.

She mustn't forget that. Hugh was angry with his mother, with good reason, but there was no doubt the other woman deeply loved him. She felt a huge wave of compassion wash over her. 'I'm going to have to go to bed. If there's any news, will you wake me?'

'I think Hugh should have rung,' Moira said, putting the top on her pen. 'He must know—' She broke off as a key turned in the front door. 'At last!'

Amy looked towards the door as Hugh came in. His face was grey. She was out of her chair in a second. 'What? Tell me.'

'Richard's fine. Well—' he pulled a hand through his hair '—not in any immediate danger. He'll need to have a bypass operation. Apparently he'd been putting it off but he's not got that luxury any more.' He sat down and stretched his legs out in front of him. 'It's been a long day.'

Amy wasn't about to dispute that. From her perspective it had been interminable. She felt as though she'd been put through a mangle. Hugh made no explanation as to why he hadn't telephoned and wasn't surprised to see his mother in his home. Amy looked from one to the other. Moira was putting her pen away in the side pocket of her handbag and Hugh had rested his head on the back of the sofa and closed his eyes. She hesitated, unsure what to do. 'Can I get anyone a drink?'

'Brandy. A large brandy.'

'Moira?' Amy prompted.

'Do you have a sweet sherry, Hugh?'

He shook his head. 'I doubt it.'

'Then a glass of wine. A small one.'

Amy walked out of the room to the kitchen. For one moment she rested her head on the woodwork of the kitchen door-frame. She made herself inhale deeply and exhale on one long, slow, calming breath. Then she straightened her back and went to open the kitchen cupboard devoted to alcohol. The brandy was easy to see. She lifted it down and found, tucked at the back, a bottle of sherry. Goodness knew how long it had languished there. She poured out the drinks and took them back to the sitting room.

Hugh hadn't moved. Amy wasn't sure whether he kept his eyes closed because he was tired or because he wanted to avoid talking to his mother. Moira was packing away the Scrabble board, shooting the letters into the black fabric bag.

'If you don't mind I think I'll go to bed. Now I know Richard is doing all right.'

Moira accepted her sherry. 'You managed to find some. How lovely.'

Amy handed Hugh his brandy. She'd so many questions she wanted to ask him—but couldn't. Not now. 'I'll see you in the morning.' His eyes flicked open but he said nothing. 'Goodnight.'

And still nothing. She turned and walked to the door, aware his eyes followed her all the way.

CHAPTER TEN

'HUGH'S already left,' Moira said as soon as Amy put her head round the door. 'He said to say he'd try and get into the office later today.'

At least that was a clear instruction, Amy thought as she poured herself out a mug of filter coffee. She couldn't have endured another day like yesterday.

'What time did he leave?' she asked as airily as she could.

'Not ten minutes ago. He wanted to get to the hospital early.'

'Ah.' He must have heard her moving about. Known she was awake and decided he'd leave without speaking to her.

She was being foolish. Of course, Hugh wouldn't be thinking about her at a time like this. What did she expect him to do?

'I'm hoping to see Richard myself at some point today.' Moira cut the top off her boiled egg. 'Hugh said he'll ring me to say when would be the best time.'

'Give Richard my love.'

'Of course.'

Amy took a quick swig of coffee. From Moira's manner there was nothing to suggest this was different from any other Monday morning. Nothing to suggest Hugh was right in assuming his mother and Richard Laithwaite had been lovers. She couldn't see any sign either that mother and son had had any kind of conversation about who his father was.

Suddenly Amy wanted to escape all the questions pounding in her head. She couldn't sit opposite Hugh's mother as she calmly spread butter on her bread. How had Hugh managed to live so many years not knowing about something so important?

She glanced down at her wrist-watch and pulled a face. 'I'd better go to work.'

'Surely you ought to have breakfast?'

'I'll grab a roll on the way.' Amy put her mug, still three-quarters full, back down on the side.

Within minutes she'd left the house and was waiting at the bus stop. Since buses on this route only ever seemed to come in threes she had a long wait but Harpur-Laithwaite was still relatively quiet when she arrived. If Richard was Hugh's father he must have loved seeing his son take his place in the company he'd founded—even if he couldn't, or wouldn't, openly acknowledge the son. But *why* wouldn't he? Richard so obviously loved him.

Amy switched on her computer and let the overnight emails appear on her screen while she sorted out the newspapers on his desk. It was strange to be here without Hugh. Amy let her fingers run along the back of his empty chair.

The door to the outer office opened suddenly. Amy's head jerked up. Startled. It couldn't be Hugh. There hadn't been time for him to have seen Richard and driven back to the office. Sonya? But why would she be here?

She walked to the connecting door and pulled it open to see Barbara Shelton flicking down the emails. 'What—?'

'Hello.' Hugh's PA looked up. 'I'm sorry to have startled you. Richard Laithwaite's assistant telephoned yesterday with the news and I arranged for a flight back down immediately.'

'Oh.'

Barbara paused to write a note on a nearby pad of paper, then looked back up. 'To tell the truth, I was pleased to get away. Four women sharing a kitchen is not easy.'

'No. I...er...I've put Hugh's papers on his desk. He should be in later.'

'Excellent.' Her hand paused on the mouse and she clicked on one of the emails. 'There's a message here from Ms Rainford-Smythe.'

Amy let go of the doorknob and came into the outer office. 'Is there?'

'Two, actually. One came through late on Friday.' Her eyes scanned the message. 'She's arriving at Heathrow at sixteen hundred hours and will meet Hugh this evening.'

Her words were like a douche of ice-cold water. *Calantha was back.*

Amy turned away, anxious that Barbara wouldn't see how much her words had affected her. She felt as if she'd been squeezed out of every area of his life—home, work and play. She wanted to scream that she wasn't ready to leave him yet. She was supposed to have a few more days with him. But the cold reality was already settling inside her.

It was time she left.

He'd phoned his mother. Calantha. It seemed the only person he hadn't spoken to was her. Perhaps nearly losing the opportunity of speaking to Richard had made him value Calantha.

The thought twisted deep inside her. It hurt so much. But nothing had changed. It wasn't Hugh's fault. It was just now she couldn't pretend to herself she didn't love him. It was only a small consolation to know he didn't suspect it.

'Do you want to take me through everything I've missed?'

Amy looked back at Barbara, seated behind her computer. It was all happening so fast. Barbara had reclaimed her kingdom.

'I kept everything on a separate disk,' she replied, hardly recognising her voice as her own. 'It's the one at the front of the box.'

There was no reason for her to be here now. By the time Hugh returned to the office she could be gone. It would probably be best. It was cowardly but she didn't want to have to listen to his explanations for resuming his relationship with Calantha. She understood. But she couldn't listen to it.

'This one?'

'Yes.'

Barbara opened the box and took out the disk as the outside line started to ring. 'Will you answer that?'

'Harpur-Laithwaite. Dr Balfour's office,' Amy said into the receiver.

'You're in early.'

Hugh. Her heart seemed to jump up into her throat, making it difficult to speak. 'How is he?'

'Richard's sleeping a lot.'

Her hand gripped the receiver so tightly her knuckles showed white. 'Have you had a chance to speak to him yet? Or—or is he too ill?'

'It's difficult to say much.' And his voice told her there were people around. Sonya, perhaps? 'But...I know my suspicions were right.'

'Oh,' she said inadequately. *So Richard was his father.* She glanced across at Barbara and knew she couldn't ask the questions she wanted to. 'That's good, isn't it?'

'He's not strong enough to talk much.'

'No, well, I suppose not.' Hearing his voice made her want to cry. She loved him so much. Knowing Richard was his father would mean he had to reassess everything in his life. She wished she could help him.

'Have you had a chance to check the answering machine and emails yet?' he asked.

'Y-yes.'

'Is there anything I need to know now?'

Amy swallowed hard. *Calantha.* He was waiting to hear from Calantha.

'If there's anything important I can deal with it from here.'

She couldn't do this. Not now. 'B-Barbara's back. She heard the news and cut her holiday short. I'll put you on to her.'

Without waiting to hear his reply she passed the receiver over. She'd tried so hard to fight her attraction for Hugh— and now she'd lost. She'd always love him. Even his voice at the end of a telephone line had her aching for him.

Amy moved away from the desk. She stood awkwardly, trying not to listen. Barbara was telling him about her family get-together, asking questions about Richard's illness. Soon she'd give him his messages. He would know Calantha was coming home.

She fixed a bright smile to her face and gestured towards the door. Barbara looked up and mouthed the word 'coffee'. Amy nodded and escaped.

In the small kitchen Amy let the kettle boil and dashed away a tear. She was being silly. Nevertheless she couldn't stay to see Hugh with Calantha. She couldn't cope with that. And if she left now Hugh need never suspect how much she loved him. She could see him at his mother's Christmas party and treat him as she always had done. They would still have a friendship of sorts. Only she would know how much it was costing.

And in time she'd forget. Wouldn't she?

*   *   *

'We should have done this months ago,' Seb said, handing her a tall glass of cold orange. 'Don't know why we didn't, really.'

Amy did. She watched the man hammer in the 'For Sale' sign outside her old home. So many memories were bound up in this place—and soon it would be gone.

She looked over her shoulder at her brother perched on the low brick wall. 'I can't believe we're doing it.'

Seb smiled. 'Any regrets?'

'Plenty. You?'

He grimaced. 'It never was my home in the same way it was yours.'

'No,' Amy agreed.

'It's the right time to do it, though. Neither of us plan on spending much time here over the next few months.'

'True.' She sipped her drink.

'And Luke's not going to come back here.'

Amy smiled across at her brother. 'It's all right. I'm not going to change my mind.' She smoothed out the creases in her soft linen trousers. Her life was in London now. She'd a new image, a new job, a new flat. She looked up and caught him watching her. 'What?'

'Did I tell you Hugh called again?'

'No.'

'You haven't called him back. What happened between you two?'

Amy sipped her orange. 'Nothing happened. I've been busy, that's all. I'll ring him some time.'

'If you say so.' Seb stood up. 'Bring your drink inside and we'll get started on packing up Mum's things.'

She nodded. Some time she was going to have to pluck up the courage to speak to Hugh. Just not now. Not while it all felt so raw. She wanted to ask her brother if Hugh was still seeing Calantha, but she didn't dare. If he said 'yes' it would kill her.

Together they walked back inside the old cottage. It smelt like a house that had been shut up. It had never smelt like that when their mum had been alive. She'd liked to have fresh flowers in large china jugs on all the wide window-sills and the scent of wild blooms had permeated everywhere. More than anything else the absence of that smell told Amy it was the end of an era. It was time to move on.

She'd dreaded this moment. Over the past few years she'd taken any excuse to avoid facing the need to get rid of her mother's things. Even her dresses still hung in her wardrobe. And what were they going to do with the china she'd loved so much but none of her children wanted? Seb's idea of selling it at auction still filled her with guilt.

'Are you okay with starting by yourself?' Seb asked, his hand resting on the newel post. 'I've put the boxes we brought down last weekend in the garage. I'll go and get them. I might even take the old bike down to the dump while I'm at it.'

'Okay. I'll make a start on the linen press.'

She didn't look back, but walked up the steep cottage stairs. There was no choice now. It was just something that needed to be done.

Like walking away from Hugh, her heart whispered. It had been the right thing to do, but the pain of it overshadowed all the lovely things that were happening in her life. He was in her mind every morning when she woke up and he was what she thought of as she went to sleep. It was as if he were in her blood, running through her veins—and there was nothing she could do to change that.

She sighed and pulled open her mother's Victorian linen press. The shelves were full of neatly folded jumpers, blouses and trousers. All exactly as she'd left them. Tiny sachets of lavender were dotted about and there was still some remnant of scent in them. It was so peculiarly evocative of her mother she felt her tears well up.

She didn't want to cry. She'd promised herself she wouldn't cry.

Distantly she heard footsteps on the stairs and she sniffed, desperate to keep her emotions together. She jerked a hand across her eyes as she heard the door behind her opening. 'I don't know whether I can do this, Seb,' she said without turning.

'That's hardly surprising,' said a voice that didn't belong to her brother.

'Hugh!' Amy spun round. For that second nothing moved. It was like a moment in time, frozen. She didn't even dare breathe. And then, 'What are you doing here? Are you visiting your mum?'

He didn't answer, merely ducking under the low doorframe to walk across and stand beside her. 'Can I help?'

Her heart was pounding painfully, pushing against her ribcage. She hadn't seen him for nearly two weeks. He looked tired. Beneath his blue eyes there were dark smudges.

'Seb's in the garage.'

'He isn't. I passed his car.'

'Oh.' Amy turned to hide her face. 'He must have gone to the dump. How is…Richard?'

'Recovering.'

She bit her lip. 'Good.'

He moved closer. 'Are you emptying out the cupboard?'

'Well, I was meant to be.' His question galvanised her into action. She leapt forward and pulled out the pile on the lowest shelf. 'We're going to decide what can be sent to the charity shop. It's got to be done. Now we've decided to sell the cottage.'

'Seb told me it was going on the market and you were doing a major clear-out today.'

'I can't imagine how we're going to get this huge cup-board out of here. The stairs are far too narrow.' She folded a white cardigan and placed it on the charity pile. 'They must have taken the window out or something. Seb told you?'

'When I phoned him again yesterday. He said you might be here.'

Her hand stilled for a second. She lifted out a second pile of clothes. 'Did he tell you I've got a job?'

'And that you've found a place to live.'

'Seb's loaned me the deposit. Probably because he wanted me off his sofa bed.' She knew she was rambling but somehow couldn't help it. Had he come to see her? 'I'm sharing a flat with three other women, one of them works at the studio.'

'So things are working out for you?'

She took out another pile of clothes and laid them on the bed. This was so hard. She wanted to ask about Richard and about Calantha. More than that she wanted to hold him. She started to organise the blouses into those for the charity shop and those for the bin. Hugh stretched out his hand and laid it across the top of hers. 'Do you have to do this now?'

'Seb—' she began nervously, but he cut across her.

'Seb won't mind.' He stopped and put his hand back in his jeans pocket. 'I need to talk to you.'

Amy glanced across at him. He was different somehow, less confident. Her fingers spread out on top of a cotton blouse. 'Did you talk to Richard?'

'Yes.'

'And?'

Hugh reached out and took hold of her hand. 'Come for a walk with me.'

'But I've got things to do. I…' Her eyes indicated the room, still full of her mother's possessions.

He pulled her towards him. 'I need you to be somewhere I know you're concentrating on what I'm saying. It's…difficult to explain.'

'Oh.' She didn't understand. Was he meaning he wanted to tell her what Richard had said? Was that why he wanted to speak to her?

The grip on her fingers tightened. 'Please, Amy.'

However scared she was about being with him, having him guess her secret, she would never be able to resist that. 'Let's go and sit in the garden. Do you want something to drink?'

He shook his head.

Amy led the way down the stairs and out through the kitchen door. Her stomach was fluttering and it was as much as she could do to stop herself staring hungrily at him.

He was unusually silent. Amy glanced back at him and found his eyes were on her. She felt herself blush. Hurriedly she turned away and crossed the lawn towards the apple trees. 'If the cottage doesn't sell quickly I suppose we ought to pick these,' she said, looking up at the fruit-laden trees. 'It's a shame if they go to waste.'

'Amy.'

'Mum used to make the most amazing apple jelly with these. I think—'

'Why didn't you wait for me to get back?' he asked softly.

Amy felt as though she'd just stepped off a cliff. There was something in his voice that frightened her. 'There was no point. Barbara was back. You know I didn't want to be your secretary.'

'Why?'

'You must be kidding?' She turned around to face him, forcing herself to smile. 'You're a terrible boss.'

'You could have waited.'

Yes, she could have waited. If she hadn't loved him so much she would have done. Amy bent down to pick up a twig. 'I didn't want to get in the way,' she mumbled. 'You had things to do. Calantha was coming home.'

He seemed to be searching for his words. 'Richard went to the same village school as my mother.'

'I know.' In a way it was a compliment he wanted to tell her the end of the story. It was difficult, though. Difficult to stand looking at his handsome face. She'd thought it had been hard not seeing him for the past ten days, but this was much worse. Now she longed to touch him, to hold him until he didn't hurt any more.

'When they met eight years later they began a kind of romance. It was very innocent. They were very young. But it couldn't come to anything. My mother's family wanted someone from a much wealthier background for her. Security, Richard describes it as.'

A soft breeze blew about Amy's face and a strand of hair flicked across her cheek. She didn't dare to move. She stood watching every emotion that passed over his face. Listening to every word he said and understanding so much more than he was saying. She could hear the pain in his voice. His desperation to understand—and to forgive.

Had he found peace?

'So she married John Balfour.'

His dad. Or the man they'd all thought was his dad.

'And Richard started as an investment banker. He says

he was driven to succeed. It was all he thought about. And then, one day, he looked up and realised he was alone. He'd set out to prove himself, make himself socially acceptable, but when he'd finally done it there wasn't anyone around to share it with.'

'That's so sad—'

'He bought a house here in Henley.' Hugh glanced across at her. 'Your mum was married then and only came back to the cottage during the summer. Luke was a baby.'

She nodded.

'And my mum was alone. Her husband had that contract in Hong Kong.'

'H-have you spoken to her?'

A shadow passed across his face. 'I've tried. She says it was wrong. It should never have happened.' He shrugged. 'She was lonely, I think. Not very happy in her marriage and Richard flattered her. Talked to her. Made her feel young. Anyway, they had an affair and the result was me. Only it was complicated because the man my mother was married to couldn't father children.'

Amy moved across and slipped her hand inside his. His fingers convulsively gripped hers. 'Has Richard always known you were his son?'

'Always.' He looked down at their hands and then back up to her face. 'He also knew my mum wouldn't leave John unless she was forced to. She'd been brought up to believe marriage was for life. She couldn't have willingly got a divorce any more than she would happily shave off her hair. She couldn't do it.'

Amy thought of Moira. It made sense of all that she knew about her. She was so concerned about other people's opinions, so certain there was a right way and a wrong way to do things.

'And John didn't want Mum to leave. As long as no one knew the baby she was carrying wasn't his.'

She didn't need him to say much more. She could fill in all the gaps herself. Her imagination was already building a clear picture of what must have happened. She could even feel some pain for John Balfour. The man who'd loved his wife so much he'd accept anything to keep her— even a baby who wasn't his own. A baby who was a living reminder his wife had been unfaithful.

Amy lifted his hand and kissed it. 'I'm so sorry, Hugh,' she said with a break in her voice. 'Does it help knowing the truth?'

'I'm glad Richard cared enough to stay in my life. I can't hate a man who has done so much for me.'

She nodded and let go of his hand. 'Did Sonya know?'

'Suspected it, I think.' Hugh passed a hand over his tired face. 'When John died Richard thought Mum might marry him.'

Amy's eyes flew back up to his face. 'After all that time?'

'But she said no. Said that it reminded her of too much pain.' He shrugged. 'I don't know, that might have been a good decision. I can't possibly say.'

'Does he still love her?'

'I don't know. I haven't asked him.' Hugh squinted up at the clouds. 'Probably. He continued building up Harpur Laithwaite and, after I'd finished my PhD, persuaded me to come to work for him. Everything else you know.'

Amy wrapped her arms round her body. 'Does Richard know about Sonya?'

A look of pain passed across his face. 'Not from me. But he knows more than I thought he did. They're getting divorced.'

'Oh,' Amy said on a breath.

'We haven't talked much about it.'

'No, well, I suppose you had other things to say to each other.' She gave him a swift smile.

He looked at her strangely. A silence grew between them and Amy became acutely aware of the sound of the leaves rustling above her head, the sound of birds and the distant hum of traffic.

'And Calantha's back,' she remarked desperately into the silence.

'Yes.'

Amy nodded. 'I read her email. Arriving at four.'

A muscle pulsed in his cheek. 'Is that why you left?'

Nervously her eyes flew to his. 'No. I—'

'Callie arrived at my house assuming we'd just pick up where we'd left off. That her being away might have made me appreciate her.'

'And didn't it?' she asked, dreading to hear the answer, but helpless not to ask the question.

A wry smile curved his firm mouth. 'I've never loved Callie. The only thing I can say in my defence is I'm certain she doesn't love me either. She'd no idea that in the time she'd been away I'd lived through a whole other lifetime. She walked into my house and all I kept thinking was, She isn't—'

He broke off. Amy didn't know what he'd been going to say. She wasn't what he wanted, perhaps? 'I'm sorry.'

'Are you?'

'Yes. Y-yes, of course I am.'

His eyes watched her intently. 'Do—do you love me?' he asked at last.

The twig in her hand snapped. 'I'm sorry?'

'Do you love me?'

There was no mistaking his question this time. Her face became heated and she longed for the ground to open up

and swallow her whole. It was so humiliating. 'I—I...
What do you mean?'

'Richard told me he thought you loved me. He said it
was in the way you looked at me.'

'D-did he?' She swallowed nervously. Her eyes fixed on
his. Her mind was desperately trying to decide what to do.
What to say.

'He also said I was a fool. And that if I kept running
from relationships I'd end up like him. He said it was a
choice you make.' He walked up close to her and his hand
gently smoothed back her hair. 'So, do you love me,
Amy?'

Her lips felt dry. Each breath she took was shallow and
painful. 'We were pretending.'

'Were we? You know, the more I thought about what
he said, the more I wondered whether he might be right.
And then you didn't return my calls and I didn't know
where you'd gone. I started to wonder whether you were
running away because you were frightened of loving me.'

'This isn't fair,' she whispered.

'I know it isn't. But I really need to know.' His fingers
buried themselves in her hair and then he bent his head
and gently kissed her. The softest, lightest touch. Against
her will Amy felt her lips move against his. *She loved him
so much.* And yet nothing had changed for her. The fear
of being abandoned was so strong.

His hands moved to frame her face and he looked deeply
into her eyes. 'I know you need to be loved. Just you. That
you're scared of marrying someone like your dad. When
you weren't at the office when I got back I thought it was
probably for the best. I couldn't be what you need.'

Amy could feel the tears begin to build up behind her
eyes. She didn't understand this. *Why was he doing this to
her?* Couldn't he just pretend he hadn't noticed she loved

him? Then they could go on exactly as they'd always done. She took another short, painful breath.

'Amy?'

She tried to pull her face away, to hide from his searching eyes. 'I can't…I don't know…' The first tear fell and she tried to brush it away.

Hugh pulled her in close. His strong arms wrapped around her and held her. Amy hiccuped and struggled to free herself.

'I love you.'

Amy felt the words rather than heard them. The tears froze on her face and she looked at him, stunned.

He thrust his hands deep in his pockets as though he didn't know what to do with them. 'I love you,' he repeated. 'I don't know how it happened. One minute you were Seb's sister and the next…' He shrugged. 'Well, the next you were different.'

She moistened her lips, scarcely daring to believe what she was hearing. 'It was the clothes. They—'

Hugh shook his head. 'It was you.'

'No.' Amy wrapped her arms tightly round her body.

'I don't know how you managed to get under my guard. I was so certain I'd got everything sorted. I'd made a decision that I'd never give anyone the power to decide whether I'm happy or miserable. It was all going so well—and then you happened. I don't like feeling out of control. And I don't like knowing that if you tell me you don't love me I'm never going to get over it.'

Amy shook her head, silver streaks on her face.

'Or that I'm going to have to live the rest of my life knowing something's missing. That it could have been perfect—but isn't because you're not there. That perhaps I missed out on you because I was too late.'

Hugh reached out a hand and smoothed away the tears on her cheek. 'Don't cry. I don't want you to cry.'

'I'm s-scared.' Her voice cracked.

'Do you think I'm not?' He looked down into her eyes. They were so frightened. Women had always been easy. He'd always had the perfect line. Known exactly what to say. But now, this time when it really mattered, he didn't know what to do. He just didn't have the words to explain the cataclysmic changes that had been going on in his life.

'I can't do this.' Amy turned and started to walk back to the cottage.

It was a moment of pure fear. He'd known rejection before, but this was going to destroy him. Nothing John Balfour had done to him had hurt like this. It was as if a branding iron were scorching an indelible mark on his soul. 'Marry me?' He'd never believed he'd say those words, but now they came out easily.

Her walk slowed and then she stopped. 'I can't.'

Hugh walked closer. 'Because you don't think I'd stay with you and that, somehow, this is history repeating itself? That I'm going to be like your dad?' He heard her sob. 'I wouldn't ask you to marry me if I wasn't certain. It's all about choice, Amy.

'When I arrived at the office you weren't there. Everything was back the way it had always been. Barbara was making me coffee and thinking of everything I might need before I'd even started to think I might need it.' He smiled. She heard it in his voice. 'And I missed you. But I kept telling myself I'd see you later.'

Amy could feel the tears burning on her cheeks. She felt as she had when her dad had told her he was leaving. She was so afraid. Paralysed by it.

'And then I went home. You weren't there either. My mother was sitting where you'd sat. And I missed you.

When Calantha arrived I thought it was you. I can't begin to tell you what that felt like. Opening the door and expecting you, only to be disappointed.'

His hands came up to rest on her shoulders and he gently turned her round. 'It was when I found you'd taken all your things I finally believed you'd gone. And I didn't know why. I was angry and hurt.' His thumbs brushed at her tears and trailed across her swollen lips. 'But I knew that I loved you. Somehow you'd managed to creep under all my defences. And I realised I didn't mind. Because I trust you.'

Amy let out a hiccup. Somewhere from deep inside her sunlight was bursting out. A gentle, warm glow of sheer happiness was beginning to spread through her body.

'I always have done.' His mouth twisted. 'I just had to learn to trust myself. What happened to you…' he stroked her face '…and what happened to me was because people made bad choices. We can choose to love each other or we can choose to walk away.'

His eyes watched her face. His eyes were so soft and understanding. Full of love. Amy slowly felt the fear recede. She could believe him. She *so* wanted to believe him.

'I love you. I've made a decision to love you. I promise you I'll live that decision every day I'm alive. But I need to know your decision. Marry me. Have children with me. Let's be a real family.'

Amy's arms stole up round his back. 'I thought you might want me for a while. Perhaps. And I couldn't do that. It would hurt too much.'

His arms tightened. 'Marry me?'

Finally she believed. Hugh always carried through what he promised. He set himself goals and he always reached them. 'Yes, please,' she whispered. She felt the emotion convulse through his body as though he'd still been in doubt of her answer. 'I love you.'

And then he was kissing her. And she could kiss him back. She let her hands travel over his broad, muscular back in a way she'd only ever done in her dreams. It was as though they'd travelled through a terrible storm and had finally come out the other side—together.

From deep within him she felt him laugh. 'You mean it?'

Amy knew her eyes were shining as she looked up into his with total trust. 'I've always loved you,' she said simply.

His arm came round her shoulder and he kissed the top of her head. 'I've got something for you in the car.'

He led her through the wicket gate and out to the front garden. Leaning into the glove compartment, he pulled out a flat, oblong parcel. Amy looked questioningly at him. 'What is it?'

'Open it,' he commanded, leaning against the bonnet.

She pulled open the ribbon and gently pulled it undone. In her hand was a black book, *his* black book. 'What?'

'I remembered what you said when we had lunch that first day and I asked Barbara for it. It was the final piece of the jigsaw. Here was my life—' he touched the soft leather '—and I didn't like it. Everything Richard was saying to me started making sense about why you'd run away from a man like me. So I thought I'd give it to you to get rid of.'

Amy felt a bubble of laughter spiral up from the centre of her body. 'Your past?'

His eyes glinted in the way only his eyes could. 'Do you want to come and chuck it in the Thames?'

'That would be very wicked. It's pollution.'

'I know. Shall we do it anyway?'

Amy laughed, clutching the book to her chest. 'What about Seb? I can't just disappear.'

'I wouldn't worry about him too much,' Hugh said, with a glance at the upstairs window. 'He knows exactly what's happening.'

'He does?' She swivelled round to look in the same direction. There in her mother's bedroom window stood Seb, his face alight with laughter. He raised his hand in recognition they'd seen him watching.

Amy glanced across at Hugh. 'How much did he know?'

'I was getting desperate.' He opened the car door. 'Get in. As soon as we've got rid of my little black book we're going home.'

Home. It was a lovely word.

Hugh fastened his seat-belt and grinned. 'Just in case you're harbouring any doubts about marrying me, I intend to make love to you until you can't think straight. You're mine.'

Amy settled herself back in the seat. 'Sounds perfect.'

His smile broadened and he leant across to kiss her. 'Let's go home.'

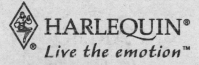

HARLEQUIN ROMANCE

**This September don't miss the first instalment
of Margaret Way's brand-new duet…**

The McIvor Sisters

These sisters get a lot more than they bargained for:
an outback inheritance, sibling rivalries—
and men they can't live without….

Brought to you by Harlequin Romance®!

THE OUTBACK ENGAGEMENT

On sale September 2005 (#3859)

Darcy McIvor is shocked at the contents of her late
father's will. He's given overall control of the ranch to
Curt Berenger, a man whom Darcy once nearly married!
When her estranged, gold-digging sister returns and starts
making a move on Curt—her Curt—Darcy knows that she'll
have to tell him exactly why she ended their affair all those
years ago…or else risk losing him forever!

Coming soon…

MARRIAGE AT MURRAREE

On sale October 2005 (#3863)

Available from Harlequin Romance

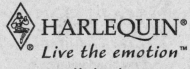

HARLEQUIN®
Live the emotion™

www.eHarlequin.com

HRTMS